Southern Blood

A MAX PORTER PARANORMAL MYSTERY

Stuart Jaffe

Southern Blood is a work of fiction. Names, characters, places, and incidents either are the product of the author's imagination or are used fictitiously, and any resemblance to any persons, living or dead, business establishments, events, or locales is entirely coincidental.

SOUTHERN BLOOD

Cover art by Katherine Perry

ISBN 13: 978-1-963517-06-4

First Edition: August, 2020
First Hardcover Edition: February, 2024

For Mom and Dan

this story only exists because of your visit

Also by Stuart Jaffe

Max Porter Paranormal Mysteries

Southern Bound
Southern Charm
Southern Belle
Southern Gothic
Southern Haunts
Southern Curses
Southern Rites
Southern Craft
Southern Spirit
Southern Flames
Southern Fury
Southern Souls
Southern Blood
Southern Graves
Southern Dead
Southern Hexes
Southern Hart

Nathan K Thrillers

Immortal Killers
Killing Machine
The Cardinal
Yukon Massacre
The First Battle
Immortal Darkness
A Spy for Eternity
Prisoner
Desert Takedown
Lone Star Standoff
The Puppeteer
Blowback
Prime

The Ridnight Mysteries

The Water Blade
The Waters of Taladoro
Waterfire

The Parallel Society
The Infinity Caverns
Book on the Isle
Rift Angel
Lost Time
Pages of Glass
The Bold Warrior
City of Infinity

The Malja Chronicles
The Way of the Black Beast
The Way of the Sword and Gun
The Way of the Brother Gods
The Way of the Blade
The Way of the Power
The Way of the Soul

Gillian Boone novels
A Glimpse of Her Soul
Pathway to Spirit

Stand Alone Novels
After The Crash
Real Magic
Founders

Short Story Collection
10 Bits of My Brain
10 More Bits of My Brain
The Bluesman
The Marshall Drummond Case Files: Cabinet 1
The Marshall Drummond Case Files: Cabinet 2
The Marshall Drummond Case Files: Cabinet 3

Non-Fiction
How to Write Magical Words: A Writer's Companion
For more information, please visit ***www.stuartjaffe.com***

Southern Blood

Chapter 1

IF MAX PORTER'S STOMACH knotted up any tighter, it would split into two and still find ways to knot up again. This wasn't the first time he had felt nervous before taking on a case, but everything about this one screamed *walk away*. A lone man — Mr. Carroll — had contacted the Porter Agency through Max's wife, Sandra. He approached her in the supermarket and said that he needed their unique skills and great discretion.

This strange tactic alone should have stopped them from pursuing things further. As the Porter Agency's reputation had grown throughout North Carolina, more and more dubious offers came their way. But something about the man intrigued Sandra, and she looked into it further. Turned out that Mr. Carroll worked as a curator for Reynolda House — the former estate of the R.J. Reynolds family that had been turned into a museum celebrating the family as well as their interest in American art. That had twisted Max's stomach even tighter.

"We have enough trouble in our life dealing with just one of the families that run Winston-Salem," Max said as he paced the polished wood floor of the Orientation Gallery at Reynolda House. "You want to take on the Reynolds family, too?"

Sandra sat on a cushioned bench as she stared at the display giving an overview history of the Reynolds family. Old black-and-white photos from 1915 showed Katherine Smith Reynolds and her husband R.J. along with their four children. Another photo from the 1950s displayed the Babcock family — one of the Reynolds daughters had married into the Babcock family and raised their children in Reynolda House during the later years. Then a photo from 1965 of her daughter, Barbara Babcock, at the ribbon cutting ceremony which opened Reynolda House to the public.

Gesturing to the photos, Sandra said, "Look at these people. It's a family whose wealth is based in tobacco. Not magic. You can relax. These are not the Hulls."

Clutching his elbows, Max said, "I don't know. Something just feels off."

"Of course it feels off. Not only from the way we were approached, but look at it now. It's Monday night, this place isn't even open on Mondays, and they want us to be here all night long. It feels like one of those movies where the crazy uncle's will gives his fortune to whoever can spend the entire night in a haunted house."

Max knew his wife tried to ease him with a little humor, but he couldn't even muster a grin. "We should leave. Tell Mr. Carroll that we appreciate his interest but whatever this is does not meet our criteria."

"We don't know that, yet. Heck, we don't even have criteria."

"We have some standards."

"At least, wait until Drummond gets back."

Marshall Drummond, ghost of a 1940s detective and partner at the Porter Agency, had scouted ahead throughout Reynolda House. If he found another ghost, he would let them know. But even if he managed to turn up a haunting, Max did not feel confident they wanted to deal with it. "It's the secrecy," he said. "I don't mean from the public. I get that the Reynolds family would not want it widely known that they hired us. But the way Mr. Carroll is handling this suggests that perhaps the Reynolds family doesn't even know we're here."

Sandra nodded with more affirmation than Max wanted to see. "That much I agree with. But we've dealt with less than upfront clients before. It happens more often than we probably would like to admit. Besides which, look at all of this — the history here is incredible. I figured you would be in love with the idea of spending a night searching through all the archives of this place, unfettered by the public getting in your way."

Max walked over to one wall with a diagram of the entire

estate as it had originally appeared — acres of farmland and clusters of small buildings with the main house drawing the eye. To the side a placard read:

> *A century ago, Reynolda operated a self-contained community of farms, villages, schools, and pleasure grounds. At its center, Reynolda House was home to two generations of the Reynolds family before opening as a museum of American art in 1967.*

It went on, and Max nodded. "Okay, I admit that this much is pretty cool."

"If you're in the mood to admit things, then why don't you admit what's really bothering you?"

"And that is?"

"Our boys. And your mother."

Max circled Sandra with the incredulous look of a police detective listening to an outrageous story by a thief caught red-handed. "What on Earth are you talking about?"

But Sandra would not let him win at that game. With a slight smile and a strong finger-pointing at him, she crossed her legs. "You know exactly what I'm talking about. The idea that PB and J are going to spend the entire night at your mother's apartment galls you."

"It does not. I mean, of course I would have preferred if we could afford a sitter to watch them all night, but they're a bit old for a sitter and we couldn't afford it, anyway. The fact that my mother even took my call is an improvement over the way she's been towards us lately, so why would I be upset?"

"That's a very good question. Been asking myself that for the last bunch of hours."

"Well, you seem to have me all figured out. What's the answer?"

"First, don't put on that pretend offended tone with me. And second, I think you don't want to owe her anything. I think you and her have fostered this anger towards each other, and you're not dealing with it."

Max turned away and saw all the stern expressions of the Reynolds family — common enough for photos from the early-twentieth century, yet somehow they felt accusatory. "Our family is in a good place. The boys look at us as their parents, not just some nice folks who got them off of the streets. We're as perfect as we can be."

"And you're afraid your mother's going to mess that up? But she took care of them for a long time. She's done just fine homeschooling PB, too."

Max could not hold back his shock. "Why are you defending her? You and my mother can't stand each other."

With a cleansing breath, she patted a spot next to her on the bench. She waited until Max sat. Then she held his hand. "Honey, it's going to be okay. I worry about the same things that you do — that your mother's going to say something or do something that will undercut all the progress we've made with those boys. Right?"

"I suppose."

"And I know you are nervous about whatever this case is. I am, too. But that's the nature of our work. We either accept it or we close up shop, and we both know that we're not going to close up. So, whatever is bothering you about your mother — the things we talked about already or something deeper than that — you need to be able to put it away, to focus on right now. It's one night. The boys will be fine. They're smart boys. Smarter than any teen I've ever known."

"You're right."

"Of course she's right," Drummond said as he rose through the floor. Dressed in his long coat and Fedora, he looked like the main attraction rising up onto a stage at the start of a show.

Max chuckled. "That's quite an entrance."

Drummond shrugged. "When you've been a ghost as long as I have, you try little things to spice up the days."

"You find anything spicy for us? Make this evening easy?"

"You expect things to be easy? What agency have you been working for? No, I didn't find anything. I suppose that's the weird part. House as old as this with as much history — I had expected a ghost or two even if they were harmless. But the only dead things around this house are the autumn leaves — and me."

Adjusting her clothes as she stood, Sandra said, "The sun's already been down for a few hours. If the ghost we're assigned to look for is cursed, then perhaps it won't make itself known until closer to midnight."

"The witching hour? Could be. Well, there's a bowling alley in the basement. If nothing else, you can kill the time by throwing a few frames."

"A bowling alley?"

"Oh, yes," Mr. Carroll said as he scurried in. "Mrs. Babcock installed all sorts of entertainments in the basement."

Short-statured and wide-girthed, he moved with the unexpected grace of an aged gymnast. He wore small wire-rimmed glasses, and his snow white goatee stood in stark contrast to his hairless head. He had a cane but did not use it with every step. When he spoke, his words came so soft and accented that Max pictured the man sitting on a porch, rocking in a chair, and sipping sweet tea on a humid North Carolina summer day.

With a strong smile, the man shook hands with Max and offered a gentlemanly bow toward Sandra. "Thank you for your patience. This is a big house, and I needed to make sure it was properly closed up for the night."

"I didn't think you were open on Mondays," Max said.

"We're not. But that doesn't mean all the doors are locked. Had to let you in here, didn't I? And though we're not open to the public, people do work here throughout the day. We have cleaning crews, our curators, people to manage the gift shop, and a whole host of others. And that's just the house. Not too far down the road we've got the gardens and the village — all once part of this grand estate. Plus, with winter nearing, if we don't lock up good and proper, the homeless sometimes try to sneak in. Not often and not on my watch, mind you, but I've heard rumors that it has happened in the past."

Sandra said, "You're the head of all this, right?"

With an embarrassed laugh, Mr. Carroll said, "Oh my, no. I only handle specific parts of the house. Mostly the top two floors, excluding the art gallery sections, but you'll see all that later."

"If you're done locking up, then, will you tell us why we're here?"

His smile faltered for a second. "Of course, of course. Follow me to my office, and I'll explain everything. That'll also help me double-check that no stragglers are stuck inside."

As he walked off, Sandra raised an eyebrow towards Max.

Drummond waved them both on. "The two of you make eyes all you want, but you know you're going to end up in that office anyway. Why bother with your suspicious looks?"

Chapter 2

MR. CARROLL LED THE WAY through the front lobby, around the corner to the gift shop, and down a flight of stairs to a hall of offices. Max swiped a guidebook from the lobby stand and downloaded the Reynolda House app, too. He found it strange how modern, utilitarian life could be attached to this preserved estate from the early 1900s. It was like two highly contrasting threads braided into one strand.

Mr. Carroll set his key at the lock of his door but paused. "I think we'll be more comfortable in the break room. My office barely has enough room for me, and I'm a fat old geezer." Chuckling, he walked toward the end of the hall, leaning heavier on his cane as its tapping reflected back. "Come on, now. Just up here."

They entered a break room that smelled of old coffee and cigarettes. Max wondered if they were still allowed to smoke in there or if decades of smoking had permeated the walls. As they sat, Mr. Carroll poured three mugs of coffee and gestured to them. Max and Sandra both accepted — they would need as much caffeine as they could get to stay awake all night.

Drummond drifted in through the wall. "I just checked the guy's office. He wasn't kidding — it's a small little cluttered thing."

"Well, now," Mr. Carroll said as he sat at the break room table. "I suppose the first thing I want you to understand is that, to the best of my knowledge, there has never been a haunting around Reynolda House." He said *haunting* as if the word were sour milk in his coffee. "The other thing I think it's important you understand is that I've only had this job a short while, and I may be exceeding the boundaries of my job description by employing you tonight."

"There you have it." Drummond clicked his tongue. "The Reynolds family doesn't know about any of this."

With a gentle tone that Sandra often used on nervous clients, she said, "Start at the beginning and tell us how we all ended up here. I promise you we've heard a lot of strange things in our time. We won't think you're crazy, and we will take you seriously."

Mr. Carroll reached over and squeezed her hand as if they were mourning the loss of a loved one. "Thank you. I've never had to deal with something like this before. Frankly, I never really believed in ghosts and hauntings until this — and I've worked at a lot of historical locations, many with rumors of hauntings, but this is something different." He shuddered.

"What makes you think this is a haunting?" Max asked.

Sandra gently nudged Max's shin with her foot. "It's okay, Mr. Carroll. Take deep breaths and tell us what you need to tell us. Take your time and put it in your own words."

Mr. Carroll did as instructed, though his deep breaths came out in short puffs. "I guess it started with small things. At least, that's how I noticed it. The first was a crack in the wall. Just in the corner of the doorjamb into one of the closets. I saw this crack snaking out into the wall. I didn't think anything of it. All houses settle over time, and cracks develop. I filled out the proper paperwork to let those who needed to know address the issue and thought nothing more of it. I remember a few days later the workers came in to properly fix the matter. Understand that something like a crack can't simply be covered over. This is a historic site and any work done to the building has to be undertaken with great care and serious consideration."

Max said, "I take it the crack did not go away."

"Very next day it reappeared. I was angry. I gave those workers more than a piece of my mind, and they had it patched up again by the end of that day. But wouldn't you know it, next morning it looked like nothing had been done. The workers apologized, but they had no idea why their patchwork was not taking."

"Then?"

"A few days later, I was here like we are right now — a Monday night, working late, and I heard banging. Sounded like somebody was hammering from inside that closet. Just trying to get out. I'm no fool. My mama taught me that whether you believe in a thing or not doesn't make it so or not so. In other words, I got the heck out of there. Drove home and tried my best not to work late at night on this property."

"But that didn't fix the matter, did it?" Sandra said.

Staring over his coffee, Mr. Carroll shook his head. "No, ma'am, it did not. For me, I had no further problems. Still couldn't get that crack fixed, but in all honesty, I stopped trying. But then one of our wonderful ladies, a woman named Lily Lee, decided she was going to work late on some of the paintings in the gallery. She keeps records of everything that comes and goes, making sure that the paintings owned by private families have the proper paperwork, and matters like that. She was here late one night when she got attacked."

"Attacked?"

His pale skin paled more as he removed his glasses and, with a shaking hand, cleaned them against his shirt. "What happened was — well, I don't know exactly what happened, but I found out about it that morning. I had come in early to get started on the day. It was Monday, so like today, we were not open to the public. I was sitting right here, enjoying a cup of coffee and getting myself in gear as they say. Lily Lee walked right through that door with a big gash across her forehead. Blood dribbling down her face. Scared the — excuse me, I almost cussed in front of you, ma'am — but she scared me good. I didn't know anybody else was in the building at that time, and of course, I didn't expect to see blood, either. Yet here comes Lily bleeding like something out of a horror movie."

Before Drummond could prod, Max said, "What time was it that you thought you were the only one there?"

"Must've been around five in the morning. Lily had to have worked throughout the entire night. This is not something we encourage nor would I have permitted it, if I had known."

Drummond said, "A lot of witching hours between midnight and five in the morning."

Mr. Carroll continued, "I set her down and went to call for help, but she grabbed me — real hard — and said I shouldn't go anywhere. Said it was dangerous in the house. So, I helped to clean her up. At that moment, I figured she was in shock for whatever happened, and once I calmed her down, I expected we'd call for a doctor and maybe I'd get some answers as to what was going on. But of course, as you can well imagine, she told me a ghost had attacked her. If she had said that weeks earlier or at another one of my jobs in the past, I would assume she hit her head too hard and knocked a screw loose. Or maybe I'd've suspected she was doing something she shouldn't and was covering up for it." He pinched his thumb and forefinger and made a little smoking gesture. "However, as it were, I believed her right away. I knew something was wrong in the house. Once she was all patched up, I sent her home for the day and got to work looking into it."

Sandra said, "You decided to face down a ghost by yourself?"

"I don't know what I decided. I don't think I was thinking all that much. I just knew that Lily Lee didn't deserve to be attacked, and it's my job to protect the people who work here. So, I went looking. Didn't find anything. I dug into the long history of Reynolda House, but nowhere is there any indication of a haunting ever. Frankly, if Z. Smith Reynolds isn't haunting this place, then nobody is."

Max did not need to know that story. He had researched the possible murder of Z. Smith by his wife, actress Libby Holman, during a tumultuous period that ended with a terrible night at the Devil's Tramping Ground. Not something Max wanted to revisit.

Sandra said, "So, you have a haunting, but you can't find out who died that would've caused it."

"Well, it could be Z. Smith," Mr. Carroll said. "I'm the first to admit that all of this is way beyond my knowledge. What I know about ghosts is, well, nothing but cartoons and campfire stories."

"And that's why you came to us."

"Yes, ma'am. Seemed like the prudent thing to do."

Screwing his face tight, Drummond thrust his hands into his coat pockets and said, "Ask him how he even found out about us."

Max relayed Drummond's question, and Mr. Carroll said, "That's Lily, again. I'm not exactly sure how she knew about you — I think a friend of a friend or maybe even another friend. Some long chain of acquaintances led to a matter that you worked on. Lily seemed to believe that not only were you the kind of people who legitimately handled these sorts of situations, but that I could trust in your discretion. That, as you might imagine, was a crucial factor. If any of this got out into the public, we'd lose everything we've worked so hard to build. The house would continue, of course, but we would then be attracting all the ghost tourists and gawkers looking for a thrill. Not the kind of attention we seek."

Max glanced at Sandra, but he needn't have bothered. He already knew she intended to take the case. The money alone would have been hard to turn down, but he had the same thought he knew rumbled in her head — *Mr. Carroll had told the truth*. Drummond appeared to have sensed it, too.

Max stood. "Well, sir, it looks like you've hired the Porter Agency."

"Oh, thank you," Mr. Carroll said, shaking Max's hand with more vigor than necessary. "I understand that one night might not be enough time, but if you can at least identify what's going on tonight, I would greatly appreciate it. We can then set up other Monday nights, if necessary, or however you want to work for us. As long as we don't disrupt the normal schedule, as long as the public is never aware of what happened, then I think we'll be fine." He looked as if Max and Sandra had already solved the case. "I suppose I should let you get to it. Here is a master key that will give you access to most everywhere in the building. I'll be back tomorrow morning, first thing, to open up for the day."

"You're leaving?" Max said.

Sandra said, "Of course, he's leaving. He knows something's haunting this place. Only crazy people like us stick around for that."

Mr. Carroll chuckled. "Even if I wanted to, I do have to go. I have a lot of work to do tonight. And, to be honest, I'm trying to see the end of *Sons of Anarchy*. I missed the show when it aired, but modern streaming is a miracle for me. Anyway, thank you, again. Good luck."

As if he feared Max might somehow strong-arm him into staying, Mr. Carroll hustled down the hall, retreating toward his office. Before Max could finish his coffee, he heard the man's rapid tapping cane as he rushed back up the stairs and exited the building.

Drummond clapped his hands together with one sharp motion. "Well, let's find out what's got him so spooked. Because it ain't a ghost."

Chapter 3

WITH A LONG NIGHT AHEAD of them, Max and Sandra agreed to take their time. Each room needed to be looked over with care, inspected closely. Not that Max expected a ghost to pop out and yell *Surprise*, but it would have been nice if the haunting went that easy. Considering the overwhelming size of the house — Max continually called it a house because it had been named Reynolda House, but really the place was a mansion — the number of rooms and items to investigate would require far more than a single night unless the ghost wanted to play nice.

First, they entered R.J. Reynolds' study. This oak-paneled extravagance was larger than the largest room in most homes. Portraits of R.J. and his wife, Katherine, hung on the walls. An assortment of chairs and a hexagonal coffee table had been placed about the room. The centerpiece of the study, naturally, was R.J.'s desk — an incredibly detailed, heavy wood piece with a lowered middle section for a typewriter.

With a hand on a metal stanchion, Max stepped over the red velvet rope keeping tourists from touching anything and closed in on the desk. "Wow. This is a real Remington typewriter. Possibly one of the first."

"What an odd assortment of styles," Sandra said as she walked around the room. "You've got Tudor paneling, these vases look Chinese, and the fireplace with all that white marble around it — I guess all the cool people were into eclectic back then."

Drummond floated over to the back corner. "Look at this."

Max and Sandra joined him around a waist-high metal smoking stand — a simple bowl on a stand used as an extremely fancy ashtray. Little horseheads curved off the sides to rest a cigarette upon and a metal piece arched over top with a dancing satyr statuette looking down at the bowl.

"If we're trying to find something that relates to witchcraft, this certainly seems to be a contender," Drummond said.

Sandra nodded. "And this is only the first room."

Max tried to imagine what it must have been like to work in this space — except R.J. Reynolds never got the chance. Reading a placard, Max said, "We knew R.J. was sick when he got here. This says he never used the study as a study at all. The family converted it into a hospital room for him. And it says over here that at one point, President Truman slept on that couch."

Drummond and Sandra looked at the burgundy leather couch. Drummond said, "That's both strange and unsettling. Feels like everywhere we turn in this room there's an opportunity for bits of odd history to poke out — the kinds of things that might lead to a haunting."

"Boys, come here," Sandra said from the adjoining hall. Something had caught her eye and pulled her a few steps out of the study.

Max entered the narrow, short hallway where he found Sandra staring at a painting on the wall. It depicted some shelves cluttered with a book and a box of odds and ends. Next to the painting, he read: *Job Lot Cheap, 1878* by William Michael Harnett (1848–1892).

"This surprised you?" Max said. "This place is supposed to be a museum of American art as well as a historical building."

With playful impatience, Sandra said, "Use a little imagination. You're an old witch, and for whatever reason, you decided the best use of your time is to lay down a curse that is going to last for generations upon generations. Now, you can curse most any object. What do you do?"

"You think this painting is cursed?"

"I know that paintings are one of the preferred objects to curse because the good ones are collected, taken care of, and can last for centuries. When you curse regular household items — a toy or a bed or anything like that — the objects often get discarded within a generation. I suspect if you were to go to the city dump, you'd find hundreds of cursed objects just rotting away. But paintings can endure."

"Yeah, and often after that they end up in museums."

From the study, Drummond said, "Why not cast a spell to see if it's cursed?"

Sandra said, "I was thinking of doing that, but there's one problem. I'm not going to draw a casting circle on this antique floor. Even if we clear away the rugs in each room or pull up the carpeting, the hardwood underneath has to be immensely valuable. Which leaves the option of drawing on the wall. Somehow, I don't think Mr. Carroll would appreciate that."

"Wouldn't you be drawing with chalk?" Max asked.

"Not for that kind of spell. Not in this situation. If we want to determine a cursed object, especially one that might be cursed by a skilled hand considering how long it'll have been around, I'm thinking something a little more permanent would be called for."

"You're not talking about blood, are you?"

"That would certainly do the trick, but no, there's no reason to go that far. I thought about nail polish, but I don't have enough to keep repeating the spell throughout the house — even if we could somehow use the stuff without ruining the walls."

"How about a pen?"

"That's where my thoughts have ended up. But that can still be so permanent that Mr. Carroll will probably have a conniption. Even if the spell works and we instantly found out what painting was cursed and we solve the case, even if we broke the curse, I don't think he'd see any of that. He'd only see pen marks all over his walls. They'd probably dock all the proper repair work from our pay. Heck, we could end up owing them money."

Shaking his head, Drummond drifted into the hallway. "I swear, the two of you can be such idiots sometimes."

"Hey, don't be mean," Sandra said with a grin.

"Sorry, doll. You're never an idiot. But your husband is a

fool."

"That goes without saying."

Max said, "If the two of you are done mocking me, how about the dead guy floating in the room explain what we're missing."

Chuckling, Drummond said, "You ever hear of a pencil?"

Sandra giggled. "He's right. It should be permanent enough to cast the spell, but with a little effort, we can erase the markings afterward. Hopefully that'll be enough to keep Mr. Carroll from losing it. I'll get started." She dug through her purse and pulled out a pencil.

Max could tell by Sandra's intensity that this would take her a bit of time. As she got to work, Max and Drummond sauntered deeper into the house. To his right, Max found another study — Katherine Smith Reynolds' small, slightly-curved room which probably had been used for more personal, one-on-one meetings. The guidebook suggested that after her husband had passed away, she often used his study for most of her actual work. Like the previous room, this one had been appointed with an eclectic and expensive taste. According to the information placard — Max had the distinct feeling he would be reading a lot of those throughout the night — in the 1930s Katherine's daughter Mary altered the hallway, making room for the current stairwell, which then shoehorned the study aside. The entrance to the study had once been a closet door.

Drummond floated through the wall and began inspecting Katherine's desk. Max left the ghost to it and turned toward the hall's other door which led to the library. Though there were beautiful built-in bookshelves, the room struck Max as more of a fancy living room. Less books and more furnishings. A sofa and chairs had been set up in front of another ornate fireplace. A piano sat in one corner. A marble bas-relief had been carved on the mantelpiece depicting Aphrodite with doves. And on the walls — more paintings. *Orchid with Two Hummingbirds, 1871* by Martin Johnson Heade (1819–1904) caught Max's eye, and he viewed it for a short time.

He settled on the edge of the couch. He did not want to sit fully back for fear of damaging the possibly priceless antique, but he had only been through three rooms and already felt overwhelmed. He needed a moment to breathe. Every piece of art, every piece of furniture, every piece of wood in the floor and hardware on the doors and cloth in the draperies hanging over the windows — everything had history. They were looking for a specific drop of soup in a vat of soup.

"Taking a rest already?" Drummond said, entering the library.

"I think I'd feel better if we had more time. If we had been hired a few days ago, I could've done in-depth research on the Reynolds family, Reynolda House, and narrowed down the most likely objects that would be cursed. But we don't even know if we're looking for a cursed object. We don't know anything."

"That's why we're here all night. Think of this like a unique kind of stakeout. Instead of sitting in the car staring at a door or a building, waiting for the bad guy to show up, we're in the building trying to find where the bad guy is hiding out. But it's still the same concept. The bad guy is here somewhere, and we just have to be patient."

"You know I hate stakeouts."

"That's because you've never understood all the best parts of this job. Now, come on partner, get up and let's check out one of the two humongous porches this place has."

Max followed Drummond into a hundred-foot long, glass-walled room called the Sun Porch. Max read that it was originally a covered carriage entrance that was later screened in and then glassed in. The view from the porch overlooked a massive front lawn which stretched nearly three-quarters of a mile. In fact, during the 1920s and 30s, those of the Reynolds family who enjoyed flying — notably Z. Smith — would use the front lawn as a runway. They'd fly out, land on the lawn, have lunch, and fly off again.

Max said, "The rich really do live in a whole different world."

"Most definitely."

"You ever see this place when you were alive? It would've been during the family's heyday."

"Oh, sure," Drummond said, the mockery in his voice unmistakable. "You know the Reynolds and me were best pals."

"I only meant that such a famous home might attract your curiosity. Or maybe you had a case here one time."

"Back then, this was just some rich guy's house, and I was a nobody detective. There wasn't a single person I knew who could get an invite to this place. Me? Not unless they were having some serious ghost problems — and as far as I know, this is the first one the house has ever had."

"That's assuming there really is a haunting going on here."

Drummond paused, hovering over a wicker chair. "Yeah, I had that thought, too. Only trouble is — I can't find an angle that Mr. Carroll would be taking if this was a hoax. I mean what does he get out of having us here?"

"Maybe he lied about not wanting the ghost tourism money. Having us here, pretending it's all secret, could be a ploy to breathe new life into the business."

Drummond tipped back his hat and shook his head. "Just because I never was in this house, just because I never knew the Reynolds family, doesn't mean I don't know anything about them. There is no way they would condone anything like that. And between the Reynolds family and the Babcock family that Ms. Reynolds married into — there's too much money, old money, to even suggest that this place needed a new source of revenue."

Max put out his hands. "Then where's the haunting?"

From the adjoining room — the Reception Hall — a pipe organ began to play *The Charleston*. Drummond clicked his tongue. "You had to ask."

Chapter 4

AS THE JAUNTY TUNE PLAYED on the organ, Max, Sandra, and Drummond entered the Reception Hall. It was an enormous room, the largest in the house, with a fireplace at the center of the back wall and staircases climbing on either side. The second floor balcony ringed the entire room. Symmetry had been built into the design with two plush couches on either side of a wide, central rug and two chairs facing each other at the fireplace. Behind each couch, a long table with two lamps and at the center, an old vase. A room like this served every possible need for the family — a play room, a place for weddings, dances, and even a concert hall. Max had once read that the viewing of R.J. and Katherine Reynolds upon their deaths had been opened to the public in this room. And back in 1951, a large spread for lunch had been set up during President Truman's visit.

But all that history of a family life could not compare to the heavy dread which played with each note from the organ. Set in the corner to Max's left, it had four keyboards tiered before the seat, and though the pipework weaved its way throughout the walls — indeed, all the way towards the top of the house with more than 2,500 pipes — the sound surrounded them.

Max watched the keys playing off by themselves. He glanced back at Sandra.

She shook her head. "I haven't finished my spell yet. This has nothing to do with me."

Drummond said, "We can tell you there ain't a ghost in sight around here. Except me."

Max walked over to the organ. He sniffed the air, half-expecting to smell sulfur or rot or some other sign of death. He smelled only wood oil.

The music stopped.

Though his heart raced, Max tried to keep a relaxed expression upon his face. "Hon, I think you should go finish that spell."

"Yeah," she said inching towards the exit. "I think you might be —"

A loud banging echoed through the walls as if someone dropped heavy rocks over and over. The lamps vibrated on the tables and even the decorative plants swayed from an unseen wind. A deep growling grew louder like an angry bear.

Max said, "Are you guys positive there's no ghost here? Because that sure sounds like one pissed off ghost."

Drummond said, "I'm telling you I don't see anything. Do you really think I'd be lying?"

The banging intensified. Max threw his hands outward. "Yeah, yeah, you can make a loud noise. It's not going to scare us. You want to be Mr. Tough Ghost? All we're seeing is somebody making a lot of noise who won't even show himself."

The sound ceased. The growling ceased.

Max looked across the room at Sandra. "I didn't think that would actually work."

"I'm not sure it did," she said. "I still don't see a ghost in here. Except for Drummond."

"Fine. So Mr. Ghost, you've gotten all quiet on us. Are you really going to be that wimpy? Make a bunch of noise, then get all silent? What kind of ghost —"

"Stop." Sandra walked to the center of the room. With a tone that mixed warmth with sternness like a parent taking charge of a child, she said, "I want to speak with the being in this house. I want to know why you are here and how we can help you. That's why we came here. To help."

No response.

With a deep breath, she continued, "There's no point in hiding from us. We're not leaving. Not until we help you move on."

The deep growl returned and fast became an enraged roar. The floor moved beneath Max's feet. If he had not witnessed all that led up to this moment, he would easily have thought Winston-Salem experienced an earthquake. As he tried to steady his balance, he felt something searing-hot pierce his skin and lift him into the air. He screamed.

Sandra stared up at him, her eyes wide and glistening with fear. Drummond shot off, swirling around Max, his hands striking at the air. As the burning pressed against Max's lungs, he patted his chest, trying to find something solid to grab onto, pull out of him, fight back against — but there was nothing.

More burning sensations shoved at his back, tossing him across the wide room. Max crashed against the far wall, cracking the plaster as he crumpled to the ground. He could hear Sandra rushing towards his side, felt her hands against him — cool and solid. The burning had gone.

He sat up, sweat soaking through his shirt as he slumped against the wall. Sandra put her arm around him and held tight while Drummond drifted towards them. She kissed the top of Max's head. "Once you're okay, I'll get back to my spell."

"I'll be fine. Get going."

Sandra held Max's head and stared into his eyes. At length, she pulled out her pencil and nodded. Before she could stand, the pencil lifted out of her hand. A startled gasp, and Sandra fell back as if shoved. The pencil rose through the air and cracked into four pieces. Each piece flew off in a different direction. The lights flickered and went out, leaving only the full moon to provide any light.

Drummond said, "I don't know what that was, but we've got plenty of proof that something is definitely here."

Max glared up at his partner. "You think?"

Chapter 5

MAX AND SANDRA BOTH pulled out penlights and flicked them on. Rubbing his back, Max stood and let the lights play across the room. Drummond produced his pale ghostly glow, yet it never reflected upon the rest of the world.

"Well," Max said, still catching his breath, "since we know this isn't a ghost, and as Drummond has so astutely pointed out, it's *something,* any suggestions as to what we're dealing with?"

Sandra walked toward the now-silent organ. "I've never seen or heard or even read about any kind of witch's curse that could do this."

"Then we're not dealing with a ghost or a witch. What else can haunt a house?"

"I didn't say it couldn't be a witch. Just not a witch's curse."

"Great. Then we're back to just knowing it's not a ghost."

Drummond said, "Sorry, pal, but we only said that we couldn't *see* a ghost. It's possible there are some kinds of cursed ghosts that are not visible to us."

Max slapped the back of the couch. "Then we can't even say it's not a ghost. Do we have any idea what this is?"

"Sure," Drummond said. "It's an angry thing that threw you across the room."

Before Max could respond, Sandra said, "Let's take one step before the next. We don't have to know exactly what we're dealing with just yet."

Max turned his penlight on her. "The bruises on my backside say otherwise."

"All I mean is that we have the entire night ahead of us and we've barely begun to explore this house. Here's what I suggest. Max and I will keep checking from room to room. I suggest we stick together — in light of the attack on you, splitting up doesn't seem too wise."

"I agree with that."

"Drummond, will you please check beneath the ground for any casting circles or corpses or such — you know what to look for. And if you don't find anything there, take a stroll through the Other and see if any ghosts there know anything."

Drummond flicked the brim of his hat. "Doll, anything for you." He disappeared.

Sandra winked at Max. "If you're done complaining about your poor little tush, shall we keep going?"

Max snorted a laugh as he walked toward his wife. "Doll, anything for you."

"Don't you start." She pushed his shoulder as they headed out of the room.

They entered the dining room — in many ways, a mirror image of the library but with the substitution of a large dark-wood dining table in place of the sofa and chairs. Numerous paintings hung on the walls, and on this fireplace, a white marble carving of the head of Bacchus, god of wine, boasted as the centerpiece.

Max kept moving around the table, flashing his penlight upon the paintings. He tried not to limp, but his right leg felt as if somebody had punched his thigh muscles over and over again.

"You got any ibuprofen?" he asked.

Sandra dug out two pills from her purse and handed them over. "You know, I've only been a mother for a short time, and I already have a full drugstore in my purse. How does that happen?"

"Family brings a lot of changes, doesn't it?"

"It's strange, but I really miss those boys tonight. I mean, we've had late-night cases before. You've been on stakeouts with Drummond, and I've had to go spend the night looking through a witch's library — but from the start, this case has felt different. I'm not talking about the way Mr. Carroll approached us or the fact that this place is haunted by some kind of non-ghost."

"I understand. I feel the same way. It's not about the case. It's about us."

"It feels like something's changed. A good thing — I think. Like it kind of hurts knowing the boys are away from us."

"There's a darker aspect to it, too. I think we are feeling unsettled because we're doing this together. Usually, if there's a late-night aspect to a case, one of us stays home with the boys. But this night, it's both of us."

Sandra looked at Max, understanding and agreement in her eyes as if unraveling a puzzle. "You think I'm worried that if we both are here, we both might not make it back. We might leave the boys alone and on their own again."

"Especially after I just got attacked. Don't you feel that way? I sure do."

But instead of a nod or verbal agreement, Sandra's brow tightened as she moved to the next room.

According to Max's guidebook, they entered the Butler's Pantry. The actual kitchens were located down in the basement. Food rose on a dumbwaiter where servers arranged the meals on silver platters and fine china. Everything then would be taken into the dining room for the family and guests to eat. The pantry stretched long and narrow. The left side had an enormous number of drawers beneath a marble counter, and glass cabinets above displayed all sorts of beautiful china and silver. In the center, a steam heating table and chrome workspace had been set up. Looked like something from an old hotel. The walls were covered in white tile emphasizing the cleanliness of the food prep area.

As Sandra opened the cabinets to check the china for witch's marks, Max leaned back against the door jamb. He watched the way she moved, the consternation on her brow, the forced swallow from her tight lips. "What's going on? What's wrong?"

"We just talked about it — the boys." She did not look over at him.

"No, no. There's something else. You suddenly look like you were the one thrown across that big room."

Carefully setting a china dish back in the cabinet, Sandra closed the door and faced Max. "It's exactly what you said — that you were the one thrown across the room. Why you?"

"I'm usually the target of these kinds of things. Maybe ghosts prefer picking on me."

"No joking. There was no reason for whatever is haunting this house to come after you. I'm the witch. I'm the one who was casting a spell. All you did was mouth off to the thing."

Max thought he missed a step or two. "So, you're worried because you didn't get thrown across the room. You wanted to be the one to get attacked?"

Sandra turned her flashlight directly into his eyes. "Don't be a jerk."

"Then what? I don't understand."

Lowering the light, Sandra walked over to Max and put her hand on his chest. "Maybe this thing could sense that I'm a witch. What if it knew that I had some kind of power?"

"You think it attacked me because I was the weakest of us?"

"Get this through your head, honey — what I'm saying is not about you."

"That's not fair. I'm trying to understand."

Sandra sighed. "Maybe studying witchcraft, even with the intent of using it for good, maybe it's changing me. Maybe at a fundamental level — one that other types of creatures can sense. What if I'm not me anymore?"

"That's quite a leap."

"Maybe. But if I'm right —"

Max wrapped his arms around her. "I promise, you are still you. I know you want to say I can't make that promise, but I can. We just proved it in the other room. We talked about the boys and how our experiences with them, our journey in becoming parents, has changed us. You now carry all kinds of emergency supplies in your purse. I know that may seem like a small thing, but it's not. It points to the fact that becoming a mom has changed the way you think at a level that you may not even be conscious of. I would call that a fundamental level." He wrapped his arms tighter and kissed her head.

She said, "Then you think my work with witchcraft has changed me, too."

"Everything we do changes us. But the fact that you ask these questions, the fact that you are trying to be cognizant of these changes, only reinforces what I've known for a while now. I've got nothing to worry about you. You are still you. You're not going to succumb to the evils of witchcraft any more than you would succumb to the evils of motherhood."

Sandra pushed back. "There are evils of motherhood?"

"Have you met my mother?"

She nestled her head back against his chest. "Good point."

They held each other in silence for several minutes. At length, they linked arms and walked back through the dining room to the Reception Hall. Max could not stop himself — he turned his light against the organ. Thankfully, it did not begin to play.

They walked to the fireplace and took the stairs to the balcony that ran the perimeter of the Hall. Though originally, the balcony functioned as a fancy way to look at those below as well as a charming gallery for family portraits along the walls — not to mention access to the bedrooms — the museum aspect of the building made the area ideal for displaying plenty of American art. With the wrought iron railing on their left, they made their way around, taking time to check out each painting they walked by. The works of Thomas Eakins, Elihu Vedder, William Sidney Mount, Eastman Johnson, and more lined the walls. Many of the subjects were portraits, a few landscapes, and one depicting two gentlemen playing cards in a dilapidated barn.

Sandra took the time to inspect each painting carefully for signs of — well, Max wasn't sure exactly what they looked for anymore. Anything out of the ordinary would do.

He regretted that thought as Sandra walked into the corner bedroom which had been converted into a furniture-less art gallery. She called out, "Come here. Now."

Hearing the shiver in her voice, Max bolted into the room. Light-painted walls covered with works of art dominated the space. That much he expected. The surprise, however — streams of blood wept from the frames around each painting. Long rivulets oozed against the walls, pooling along the floor molding and into the carpeting.

Standing in the middle of the room, her eyes open wide as she gazed from one painting to the next, Sandra said, "I think we may have found the source of the problem."

Chapter 6

TINGLING WITH THE URGE to rush across the room, grab Sandra by the hand, and yank her to the relative safety of the balcony, Max watched his wife closely. He clamped his mouth tight against blurting anything out — she clearly concentrated on the paintings. It would not only be bad form, but it could be dangerous to break the focus of a witch at a time like this. And she was a witch.

That thought echoed through to the center of his chest. It simultaneously hollowed him out and filled him up. It frightened him even as it warmed his heart.

In a calm almost casual manner, Sandra said, "Don't touch anything."

After a few moments, it became clear that they would not be leaving this room anytime soon. She continued to move from painting to painting, checking each one for some unseen marks or symbols or other aspects that Max did not understand. When she finished her circuit, she began again. Unsure of how long they would be, Max settled on the floor just outside the doorjamb — nobody wanted to sit in a blood-soaked gallery — and he pulled out his phone.

Might as well further his research on the place.

Of course, with a family as famous as the Reynolds and a location as iconic as Reynolda House, the amount of information available threatened to overheat his phone. However, he could quickly dismiss most of it as rehashing the same facts over and over.

Katherine Smith Reynolds had gone down in history as a remarkable, kindhearted, wonderful woman who always showed great appreciation for the wealth she enjoyed. Whether it came from little things such as the fact that she insisted all the staff eat the same meals that were prepared for the family to the larger decisions such as how to run the house itself — a modern version of a country estate. She worked actively in the community to help those in need and promote the rights of others. Though Max felt sure if he dug deep enough, he would find a human being as flawed as any other, he did not uncover anything that would hint at the idea of Katherine Smith Reynolds being involved with witchcraft.

Max glanced into the gallery. The blood no longer flowed from the frames and had begun to dry up on the walls. Sandra stood before one painting, rigid with her head tilted back like an art critic observing a new piece for the first time.

He returned to his own work. R.J. Reynolds proved no more suspicious than his darling wife. However, being a tobacco tycoon meant that he had created many enemies throughout his life. Pictures of him presented an imposing figure with a thick, Southern beard and a strong, heavy glare. But the man did have the sensibility to marry Katherine, and she clearly had an influence upon him. No — Max did not see any hints of witchcraft from the husband's side, either.

Besides, if either Mr. or Mrs. Reynolds had been dealing with witchcraft, evidence would have turned up long ago. Max and Sandra had been involved with witches for too long now not to have come across even rumors of such a notable couple being connected to that world. Heck, Max's first employer in North Carolina had been the Hull family — the actual controllers of witchcraft for many decades before. Surely, they would have known and disapproved of the Reynolds family having a hand in their affairs. Probably would have led to a war between Hull and Reynolds.

There was the possibility that somebody had cursed the Reynolds family, but again, too much time had passed. What was the purpose of this curse if it only came to life now — over a century after R.J. Reynolds had died? And any curse during R.J. or Katherine's lifetimes would have become the stuff of legend within the witch community. But Max had never heard a word.

Even the most cursed member of the Reynolds family — Z. Smith Reynolds — could not be linked to witchcraft. The man lived an adventurous life, one filled with many unfortunate choices and an untimely demise, but Max's previous research on him for another case had turned up nothing.

Sandra's voice cut into his thoughts. "The paintings in this room aren't from this house, right?"

Max pulled up the Reynolda House app on his phone. "That's right. These bedroom galleries showcase different artists at different times of the year. Most of the paintings on the walls that we've seen throughout the house either belonged to the Reynolds family or were bought by the family as permanent parts of the museum. At least, it seems that way. But these galleries — yeah, many of these paintings are only being displayed and are not even owned by Reynolda House. Why?"

"Not sure yet."

Since Sandra was talking, Max thought he could speak without interrupting her train of thought. She would tell him otherwise, if that was the case. Rising to his feet, he rolled his shoulders and took a step into the room. "I've been looking through the family history — nothing suspicious there. But now I'm thinking about Cecily Hull."

"Oh?" Sandra said, shifting sidewise to look over the next painting.

"She's the only new player in anything right now. Perhaps she's leading a new attack against the Reynolds family."

"Why now?"

"Maybe she figures striking at the Reynolds family will help solidify her control over the witch world. Show her strength and power."

Sandra's attention did not leave the paintings. "No. She and Madame Ti have been clamping down on the witches harder than expected. At least, that's what I'm hearing on the witch boards online. The old guard at the Hull family sure made it look easy, but witches are a bit anarchic at the core, so they're not inclined to follow anybody just because of the name Hull." Biting her lip, she said, "Do you remember a case from long ago about an art forger?"

He snickered. "We haven't been doing this long enough for me to forget any of our cases. Especially one about an art forger who was two hundred years old and his crazy daughter trying to resurrect Blackbeard the Pirate — I doubt I'll ever forget that one."

Sandra indicated one painting situated near the middle of the far wall. It depicted a pastoral scene of a young man plowing a field by hand. Sandra brought her face up close. "Look at this one. I don't think this one fits with the others."

As Max strolled over, he said, "They're all pictures of the land and farming and animals."

"Stop joking around and take a look at this."

Max brought his face closer to the painting. He frowned. Then he looked close again. "Are these all supposed to be by the same artist?"

Sandra checked the placards next to each painting. "Yes. Sylvia Martin."

Max shifted to the painting neighboring the plowing man. He looked closely at the texture to confirm his suspicion. Stepping back to the first painting, he said, "Unless Ms. Martin severely changed the way she paints, I think you're right. This is a forgery."

"It's the smoothness, right?"

"Yeah. In all the other paintings, Ms. Martin really puts on the paint thick. It's like looking at a topographic map. But this — the style looks the same, but the actual brushwork is different. Huh. Didn't think I learned so much during that case."

Sandra reached forward and gripped the painting by the frame. She hesitated, long enough for Max's stomach to wriggle, and then she removed the painting from the wall.

They both glanced at the backside. Nothing. Meeting each other's eyes, they shared concern before turning to look at the wall. A bloodied handprint surrounded by a circle of blood had been pressed into the wall. Like the graffiti tag of a madman.

Without thinking, Max reached up and touched the mark. Like a receding echo, he barely heard Sandra cry out, “No!”

Chapter 7

THE WORLD FELT FUZZY AND COARSE like the ends of a frayed rope. Max turned back, but he could not see Sandra. The paintings, the blood, the handprint — all gone. A light flickered from the balcony. It had a strange color — ghostly pale yet warmly amber.

Feeling drugged — *or,* he thought, *maybe this is what a trance feels like* — Max walked out onto the balcony. Standing by the stairs leading down, he saw a man — early 30s, average height, dark hair, and a face that chilled Max's skin far colder than passing through any ghost. He knew that face. He had seen it in photographs. He had it described to him through countless memories. A face that belonged to someone he knew for a short time in his early life but should have known much longer.

Through his constricted throat, Max managed to say, "Dad?"

The organ began to play. Not the upbeat playfulness to dance the Charleston, but rather a somber tune. Not really a tune even — more of an emotion. Like the kind of ambience music found in a movie during a scene in which the music only added to the emotion but was not meant to draw attention to itself. Even as Max had that thought, his focus turned back to his father descending the stairs. The organ music continued to play, but Max barely registered it.

As he descended, he smelled the delicious aroma of a full banquet. He heard the clinking of dishes and the chatter of countless voices. Not loud. Not overwhelming. But like the organ music, they tinkled in the background no more than distant wind chimes. At the bottom of the stairs, Max spotted his father standing by the fireplace, holding an ax on one shoulder as if he had just returned from chopping firewood. As Max stepped closer, his father turned away.

"Where are you going?" Max asked. "What are you even doing here?"

His father paused to look back. "What I should've done long before I went away. Teaching you the truth of things."

Before Max could ask another question, his father turned left and walked out of view. Max followed.

He entered the back porch, also called the Lake Porch, which covered a long portion of the back much like the Sun Porch covered the front. However, the original design had eight large columns holding up the roof in a semi-circle. Thankfully, over the years, the porch had been enclosed with giant sheets of glass. Were it daylight, he would have been able to see all the way across the land toward a wetlands which had once been a sixteen acre man-made lake, Lake Katherine. But it was nighttime. Max only saw his own reflection in the glass and darkness behind. To his left, standing before yet another fireplace — this one bracketed by two maroon couches — Max's father stared back.

Max wondered how he could see his father, let alone anything in the huge porch, with the night so dark. He should have brought his flashlight with him. Did he leave it in the upstairs gallery?

He turned toward the Reception Hall, thinking he should run back upstairs, but his foggy mind cleared enough to remind him that his father stood in the room with him. His father. Who cared how he could see the man? He *saw* the man.

And for some reason, his father held the ax at his side. Blood covered the ax head and had splashed upon the man's pants.

"Dad? What's going on?" Max approached in halting steps. "What did you do?"

As he neared, lightning flashed — there wasn't even a storm. In those pale flickers of light, Max saw Sandra, PB and J, and his mother strewn about like a horrid jigsaw puzzle. Blood covered the white walls and white-tiled floor. It looked as if somebody had tossed red paint throughout the Lake Porch. Limbs scattered in one direction, torsos in another. And placed on the two couches like a psychotic display were the heads of his loved ones.

"What have you done to my family?" Max said, tears streaming down his face. "My perfect family."

In a scratchy voice as if he had crawled out of the grave, his father said, "No. Not perfect. Especially your mother."

"How could you do this?"

With a sickly glint in his eye, Max's father cocked his head to the side and grinned. "How perfect could your family be? Your own mother ran off your father. He couldn't take her henpecking. And you — he had no interest in you."

Max wanted to argue, wanted to defend his mother, his life, but his body refused to obey. He stood there frozen like a five-year-old that knew something was wrong but lacked the power to do anything about it.

Dragging the ax head along the floor, letting its metal scrape against the white tile, his father said, "I know what you're thinking. Part of you doesn't believe I'm here. Part of you thinks this is all in your head. But I know things you don't. Because you never knew me. Not really. Though you might have some snippet of a memory — maybe a summer day in the backyard splashing around in a plastic kiddy pool. Or maybe you remember a birthday with your mother baking a crappy little cake, and there I am standing in the corner with my arms folded, forcing a smile to all the other parents. But if you really think about it, if you really dig deep, you'll remember why you never wanted to dig deep in the first place. Because I'm not there. You'll never have a perfect family because you've never known what one is. You think you could be a father? You and that wife of yours should've stuck to your guns and never had kids. Neither of you are fit to be parents. What kinds of parents leave their kids overnight with an unstable, overbearing woman like your mother?"

Max shivered. He could ignore most of what his father had said — at least, he thought he could — but this last point struck hard. They were supposed to protect those boys. As parents, they were supposed to watch out for the boys and not put them in bad situations. But from the start, they had done just that. They had used the boys on cases, and they had relied upon Max's mother to watch the boys when it was inconvenient to do the watching themselves. Heck, they entrusted PB's education to Max's mother.

"Look at that," his father said, blood dribbling from the corner of his mouth. "I can read it on your face. All this time, you had convinced yourself that you were going to be the father I wasn't. You and your cocky little brain thought you could do so much better. Not so easy, though, is it? Not when your mother's around. You blame me because I failed you, and I did, but not because I left. Not because I wasn't there to wipe your stinky ass while you were learning to get out of diapers. Not because I wasn't there to smack you upside the head when you said something stupid as a teen. No, no, my son, I failed you because I didn't have the strength to do what I should've done with your mother." He hefted the ax back on his shoulder spraying an arc of blood across the floor. "If I had simply hacked her to pieces back then, we would never have suffered under her. I would still have left — don't think for a second I wanted you — but the state would've put you into better care. Just look what's happened to your boys — the state let you take care of them. Oh, that's right, not such a good idea."

"Shut up. I don't know who you are."

"Of course you do. You knew it the moment you saw me."

"I don't care. You've never been part of my life, and you're not going to start now." Max wished his fingers did not shiver at his sides. At least, he now spoke — even if he sounded more whiny than self-assured.

"I know it's frightening. The truth. The mere idea that you have failed before you even started. It's hard to take."

"Stop it."

"That's for you to do. You can end the suffering of your wife and your children. All you have to do is the thing that I failed to do. You can even use this ax, if you want."

"I won't listen to you."

"You already have. You understand. The fact is that if you want that perfect family for your wife and your boys, then your mother's got to go."

A hesitant voice spoke from behind. "Max?"

He whipped around with the relief of finding a life ring in the ocean. "Sandra." He rushed over and embraced her. Squeezing, he heard the air press free of her lungs.

"What's going on?" she asked. "How did you end up down here?"

Dark shrouded the Lake Porch. Sandra's penlight flashed around, and Max saw the white columns and the clean floor and the lack of bodies. "It wasn't real," he whispered. From his pocket, he found his own penlight and searched every bit of the Lake Porch. Most of the space was empty, but he had to check. He had to know for sure that there was not a single splotch of blood anywhere.

With forced calm, Sandra said, "Let's go into another room. We should sit down, and you can tell me all about what happened. Drummond's back. He can join us, too."

Trying to slow his hammering heart, Max nodded. "Sure. Let's do that." As they walked toward the exit, however, he noticed an ax leaning against the fireplace.

Chapter 8

MAX SLUMPED AT THE HEAD of the dining room table with Sandra by his side. She clutched his hand as he told the story of what had occurred, and her eyes never left him. Even as tears trickled down her cheeks.

At one point, he tried to flex his fingers, but she would not let go. While he appreciated her loving concern, he didn't understand why she reacted so strongly. Until she wiped her face with her free hand and said, "That's all you remember?"

"That's not enough?"

"Hon, you've been gone for hours."

It hit Max like a heavy rope rippled with barbed knots — one statement and the painful thuds worked through his bones. "What are you talking about?"

Sandra explained that when Max touched that handprint, something happened to her as well. She did not realize it at first — at one moment, Max reached toward the symbol and she cried out *No,* and the next moment, she stood in the gallery without him. Feeling off — sort of drugged — she tried to piece together events, but nothing made any sense. When she finally pulled out her phone to text Max, she discovered the time — midnight. The witching hour.

Drummond floated into the dining room. "I've looked all over that porch, and I'm telling you, there's nothing. No sign of a ghost, no residue of magic having been used, no witch symbols. Nothing. Not even this ax you were talking about."

"Nothing at all?" Max said, the desperation in his tone sending a shudder down his back.

"Sorry, partner. But I can't say I'm too surprised. I've checked under the house, above the house, around the house, and I can't find a single thing out of place. No bones, no curses — there's simply nothing wrong here. And before you ask, yes, I went into the Other. But everybody from the Reynolds family has moved on long ago. Even the worst of them, the most likely to be cursed, they all accepted their fate. None of them were stuck hanging around. And none of them were forced into it by a witch's curse."

Max's fingers curled into a fist and dropped with a dull thud on the table. "What are we going to do? I'd research something, but I have no idea where to begin."

Sandra released his hand and kissed his cheek. "For starters, I think it's important that this happened at the witching hour. When you touched that handprint, I don't know exactly what time it was, but we hadn't been in the building all that long. Even if we were here for two hours, it would still have been around nine o'clock. Yet we both did not return to our senses until the witching hour. That's on purpose."

Drummond said, "Only problem with that idea — Max got attacked in the Reception Hall well before any witching hour."

"I didn't say this thing could only work at the witching hour, but clearly, it prefers that time. Maybe it's stronger then."

"Throwing Max clear across a room isn't strong enough?"

"But at the witching hour, it manifested as his father." She checked her phone. "It's now twelve-thirty. We've got two-and-a-half hours until the next big witching hour."

"To do what?"

Sandra pushed back from the table and paced the length of the dining room. As she spoke, Max had to admit that part of him thrilled at watching her. She always managed to find the strength to be his rock when he needed it. When he was down, she was up, and together they created a balance in the world for themselves. When he felt tied up, she was there to untie them. At the moment, his brain had tied so tight he could not find where to begin.

"What do we know?" Sandra said. "This thing is active on ground that has not been cursed or touched by any magic that Drummond should be able to find. We know that this thing is fixated on Max."

Drummond said, "It clearly can get into a person's head and pray upon their deeper fears. Unless Max has been blabbing about his father for the last bunch of years and I somehow missed it."

"And we know that somebody is behind this. Somebody in the living, physical world."

Max said, "We do?"

"Unless ghosts can start forging art, then yes."

Tapping his chin as he drifted in both thought and form, Drummond said, "Who would set up a trap like that? There's no way it could have targeted Max."

"That's my point. Whoever's trying to screw with Reynolda House would have no idea that Mr. Carroll had hired us."

"Which means the culprit set the painting there knowing that Mr. Carroll or Lily Lee or some other person working in this building would notice it, wonder what it was doing there, take the painting off the wall, and find that handprint. They were supposed to touch it and get whisked away to whatever horror their brains led them."

Max said, "That's all possible, might even be right, but where does that get us?"

Sandra shrugged. "I'm just trying to think this through."

Standing, Max's mouth formed a tight line. Something Sandra had said picked at the muddle in his brain. "If we set off this bit of magic by accident — because it was meant for somebody else — then why did it show itself to us in the first place? The bleeding frames and everything? I mean, if you were to curse a group of people or a house, you wouldn't want your big, show stopping number to happen for the wrong people. Right?"

Sandra snapped her fingers. "Except that many of these types of things can't differentiate between one person and the next. Not without more distinct magic like a casting circle — which our dear partner, Drummond, has said there isn't one."

"So, we're suggesting that somebody set this in motion without any care for who got hit. Like a mine in a warzone.

You don't care who triggers it, as long as it's the enemy."

"Except instead of a mine, this thing was unleashed."

Max rubbed his face. "If we had more time." He wanted to go to the library and dig up old records of the estate. Maybe there was some reason to want this building shut down.

"Hon," Sandra said. "You should calm down. If this is like any type of creature a witch could create, it will feed off of negative energy."

"But we know a witch didn't create it. There's nothing that shows us anybody created it. Not really."

"Magic as a whole is merely a harnessing of the natural energies that surround us. Since this thing did not attack me and went after you, and based on the experience you had in the Lake Porch, I'm thinking it's feeding off your negative energy."

Drummond pointed at Max like a huckster. "You see? All your negativity comes back to bite you."

Max flipped off the ghost.

"Great. More negativity."

Sandra said, "Two-and-a-half hours. That's all we have. We need you to be brutally honest. Because if we get to the next witching hour and you withheld something, if you're still harboring this negativity, then that thing will come after you again. I don't want to know what it'll do to you the later things get. So, out with it — what's troubling you?"

Chapter 9

THE PORTRAITS IN THE DINING ROOM all stared at Max with accusing eyes as if souls from long ago reached out from the walls pointing their fingers. Max clasped his elbows as he looked from Sandra to Drummond. "What? I'm not holding back anything."

With a soothing tone that made Max think of a psychiatrist, Sandra said, "I know how important our family has become to you. Especially after everything that went down with PB and his father. We have fought for those boys. Are you afraid we're still going to lose them?"

"There's nothing wrong with the boys. We're not going to lose them. We may not be the most perfect of perfect parents, but were pretty darn close. We have an unusual job, that's all. It creates unusual circumstances."

"Ah."

Max flailed out one hand. "Don't *ah* me. I know what that *ah* means. I know what you're thinking."

Drummond said, "Well, I don't. What am I missing?"

Max stormed closer to Drummond while pointing a finger back at his wife like a prosecutor in a murder trial. "She's trying to say that this is my mother's fault. Isn't that right, hon? You think that we wouldn't have any of these problems without my mother. That I should just get rid of her."

As Drummond's eyebrows raised, he gazed down at Max with a pitiful click of the tongue. "You got all of that from her saying *ah*?"

"She wants brutal honesty. Well, my wife has never liked my mother."

Sandra said, "We're making progress. Slow progress, but we

are moving forward. Even if we never got along, even if she hates me to my dying day, I would never suggest that we get rid of her. I know how important she is to you."

"Do you? Because as good as we have it right now with our little family, as good as those boys have it being with us, I didn't have any of that growing up. If it wasn't for my mother, I'd have had even less. My father — my real father, not that abomination from the Lake Porch — I never knew him. He was gone before I could even think about him. She raised me by herself, while holding down a job to keep food on the table, making sure I got an education, making sure everything that I needed was there. She wasn't perfect. She wasn't an angel. You've heard me complain about her plenty of times. But that doesn't mean I don't respect her. It doesn't mean I don't owe her."

Sandra paled as if Max had physically struck her. "I'm not denying any of that. Nobody here is suggesting she isn't important."

"That thing in the Lake Porch is. And if it's feeding off my energy, then it's feeding off my thoughts. So you explain to me why it's suggesting the solution to our family being perfect is to cut her out of the picture."

"Listen to yourself. All that negative —"

"Stop with all that negativity crap. I'm just angry."

"Anger is a result of fear. Until you get this, deal with this — your mother — all that anger will feed whatever's going on here."

"She's right," Drummond said. He lowered to the floor and removed his hat. Scratching the back of his head, he cleared his throat. Max saw the earnestness on his partner's face, and it dammed his flood of rage. Clearly, whatever Drummond wanted to say, the old ghost had to build up to it, build up the courage. More than anything, that fact twined its way through Max's chest.

"You know, I had an absent father, too," Drummond began. "I don't like to talk about him because I never really knew him. I mean never. He got my mom pregnant by accident, was forced into marrying her, and did as little as possible to be my father. But I would learn over time that he always ran from his responsibilities. Even volunteered to fight in World War I just to get away. I also know about owing and respecting troubled mothers."

He paused. Long. So long that Sandra moved to his side and reached up as if she were going to pat his shoulder, only to remember that she could not touch him. "She was institutionalized, wasn't she?"

"I did the best for her I could. But even the best facilities back then were not wonderful places to be. Not unless you had ridiculous amounts of money — like the kind of money to build this house. Still, she did her best for me, and I made sure that when our roles were reversed, I did the best for her. So I understand why it's important for Mrs. Porter to be well taken care of."

"Thank you," Max said.

"You know, having a family — any family — is a difficult thing. But it's not based on how many people you've got. We don't keep score. When it was just you and Sandra, you had a family. I had a similar thing once in my life with this waitress. Long ago. She had her own children, her grandmother — her *abuela* — and it was for just a short period. I know now that it would never have worked, but there was a moment when the whole thing packed into this little sphere, and nothing could stop us from being together. I'm not talking about the lust or overly romantic way you feel at the beginning of a relationship. I'm talking about that sense of family."

"That's exactly it. I'm trying to protect that."

"That's the thing," Drummond said, leveling his ghostly gaze at Max. "You can't control how a family takes shape. You can't control any of it. All you can do is play your part and enjoy the good moments that you get. I know this because I had it once with my mother — just the two of us. I had it once with this dear waitress. But I never understood it. I never appreciated what I had. And I only know that because I have it again. Now, with you. I mean, for crying out loud, I even like those kids."

Sandra burst out a sound somewhere between a cry and a laugh. Max's body stopped responding in the shock. At length, he said, "I guess we are a family."

"All I'm saying is that whatever flaws we have, whatever struggles you feel about this family, we are all in it together. We all want to keep close and united. So, there's no need for you to feel this negative energy. Especially in this house."

Sandra beamed a grateful smile at Drummond. More than anything, that smile made Drummond's words true for Max. The old ghost really was part of their family.

Lights flashed through the front porch windows. Max looked over to see a car winding up the drive. "What's this now?"

Setting his hat back on, Drummond said, "Oh, yeah. Thought we could use a little help. After I was in the Other, I swung by and convinced a friend to pay us a visit."

"What friend?"

"Irene Beck."

Chapter 10

LIKE THE POLICE, the Porter Agency had its share of run-ins with psychics. Sometimes it seemed that every other month brought a new one to their door. These folks — some well-intentioned, some scam artists — offered their services to help Max and Sandra speak with the dead, find a missing body, or understand the spiritual essence of their enemies. Of course, Max could already talk with one dead ghost and Sandra could talk with all of the dead. They had no need for sussing out which psychics truly held power and which truly held delusions. But during one case involving the Winston-Salem Fire Department, they met Irene Beck.

She was a short, stout woman with a big voice and a bigger drawl. Her strong confidence and charm ran as deep as her Southern roots. Most importantly, in addition to being an authentic psychic, she had become Drummond's friend.

"Hi there, Sweet Cake," she said, gazing up at Drummond as she entered the Reception Hall.

Perhaps more than a friend. Max did not wish to poke into Drummond's private life. He figured the less he knew, the better. Still, he couldn't help but snicker. "Sweet Cake?"

"Because he's just all sugar."

Drummond tightened his coat and leveled his eyes upon Max, daring any further response.

Irene walked right by them and focused on the pipe organ. "This is where it all started, right?"

"That's right," Sandra said.

Max broke away from his face off, and they all joined Irene. "It started playing itself, and then we tried to talk to this thing — whatever it is. Well, that thing didn't like what we had to say, so it picked me up into the air and tossed me clear to the other side of the room."

Irene's eyes traced a path in the air to where Max had fallen. He found it difficult to read her expression — some blending of excitement and intimidation, perhaps.

Drummond said, "It's like I told you — we've looked all around, even under the ground, and we can't find any sign of a ghost or a curse. Until Sandra discovered that bloody handprint up in the gallery, we couldn't point to anything."

"If you want," Sandra said, "I'll show you where it is."

Irene patted her chest and chuckled. "Oh my, all y'all are acting like a bunch of hungry hens about to get fed. Making so much noise and fluttering all about. Everybody needs to calm down. Now, I've worked with other paranormal investigators, too. Those ones don't have the benefit of a friend like Drummond, so they have to deal with things in a more structured manner."

Max tensed. "Don't go comparing us to a bunch of camera hogging ghost hunters trying to get on television."

"Watch yourself. Not everybody in this business is looking to become famous. Most of them, in fact, are simply trying to understand the paranormal world that they have glimpsed. Your little group is unique, and you ought to respect that. Your wife — with her own psychic abilities and her own connection to witchcraft — why she alone makes this outfit special. You throw your own private ghost detective into the mix, well, you have a leg up on everybody else in the state, probably in the country. But what you don't have, what you need me for, is the wealth of knowledge about all the things greater than you in existence. Especially, those which I have personally experienced. Now, I've come all the way out here as a favor to a friend. Do you want my assistance or should I turn around and leave?"

Max did not have to look at Sandra or Drummond to feel their disapproving eyes on his back. With a sheepish nod, he said, "My apologies. We've been at this for a long time already tonight, and I suppose I'm a bit on edge. I meant no offense."

Smiling thick enough to hide any undercurrent of irritation, Irene said, "None taken. Now, as I was trying to say, we're going to approach this in a simple and logical order. In that way, we can discern what this thing is not, and hopefully, narrow down what it is. Because of your uniqueness, we already know that this is not a ghost. That's good. That'll save us many long hours of work. Likewise, to the best of your knowledge, there is no casting circle or other evidence of a witch's curse. Any other entity out there is most likely going to be less obtrusive than a ghost. No offense, Sweet Cake."

"I agree. Some of the ghosts I've known butt into all kinds of things where they don't belong."

"So, what we are going to do right now is sit down in this enormous and lovely room and be quiet. We will listen." With that, she meandered over to one of the wide couches and scooted onto the end.

After standing in silence for more than a minute, Max decided it made more sense to sit. This process would clearly take some time. Besides, his back ached from the abuse he had endured.

He picked the couch opposite Irene, and Sandra soon joined him. Drummond opted to float near the ceiling and observe from above.

Within minutes, Max wanted to stand, wanted to pace around, wanted to at least tap out a rhythm on his knees. He glanced up at Drummond. The ghost watched his psychic gal with intense focus. Sandra appeared to be relaxed — waiting as if settling in with a good book and no cares to trouble her mind.

But not only did Max worry about the thing within these walls — the entity — he also worried about his own thoughts. If Irene took much longer, he would start to ponder the conversation her arrival had interrupted. He would think about Drummond and Drummond's father and what the old ghost had meant by sharing that part of his life. Beyond the obvious.

Recognizing that he'd already begun to roll down that dangerous path of thought, he cleared his throat. "Sorry to interrupt, but you should know we're on a time crunch here. The next witching hour isn't that far off and —"

"Shush," Irene said.

Max closed his mouth. With a scowl and a shake, Irene hopped to her feet and entered the Lake Porch. Everyone followed.

As she slowly walked through the porch, each foot placed carefully as if she navigated a minefield, she eventually settled on a soft cushioned chair. Closing her eyes, she sighed and listened.

Max maintained a distance, keeping back near the entranceway. He did not want to step any further than necessary into this part of the house. Pressing against the wall, he kept his eyes lowered, staring at his feet. He did not dare look up. The idea that he might see his father standing there, splattered in blood, with that sadistic grin on his face — Max's stomach churned.

Or the ax.

What if Max looked up and saw that ax leaning against the fireplace? What if he moved any closer into that room and his mind grew fuzzy and the next thing he knew, he held that ax, and the blood splatter covered him and —

"Perhaps we should go into a different room," he said. "We can tell you what happened here so that you might be better prepared to sense the things you're looking for."

In unison, Sandra and Irene said, "Shush."

Irene struggled to return to her serene moment, but the frustration on her tightening features suggested she could not. With a roll of her shoulders, she pushed off the seat and returned to the Reception Hall. When the others followed, they found her already climbing the stairs. Max knew exactly where she headed. Sure enough, she walked straight for the gallery.

When he stepped in, he could not believe how clean the room appeared. Not a drop of blood on the walls, on the floors, in the carpet. He looked to Sandra, and she shrugged. At least, that much acknowledged that he had not imagined the blood. But it did little more to ease his mind. Especially because the bloody handprint no longer marred the wall. In fact, only the forged painting sitting on the floor provided any evidence that he and Sandra had experienced anything at all.

Irene walked to the center of the room and inhaled deeply. Like a yoga instructor, she calmed her breathing and closed her eyes once more. With her arms at her sides, she stood motionless.

Max wanted to stomp off along the balcony, put more distance between him and the gallery, but he didn't want to leave Sandra. The games being played with his mind only jumbled his thoughts more. He did not want to think about the little psychic. He did not want to think about any of it. Because the more that the evening spun in his head, the more tension he felt. Even anger. With an audible huff, he said, "Perhaps if you tell us what —"

Irene said, "Shush."

Sandra said, "Be quiet."

Even Drummond spoke up. "Let the woman do her work."

A heavy silence followed. Max wore that weight like a yolk keeping him in place. He tried to clear his mind, hoping that he could push aside his concerns about Irene. But she simply went from one room to another, following their previous encounters, offering nothing new.

Until her eyes snapped open. She brushed by Max as she exited the gallery. Out to the balcony, she moved toward the narrow stairs winding up into the attic.

With her hand on the rail, she turned to Drummond. "You've been up there?"

"Dear, I've been everywhere in this house."

She locked eyes with Sandra and then Max. "I'm feeling a lot of energy from up there."

Sandra stretched to see ahead. "Then we go up."

Irene did not move. A slight incline of her head indicated that she would not lead the way. Before Max could storm forward, Sandra took the first steps. Irene followed, and Max and Drummond brought up the rear.

Halfway up, Irene Beck let out a horrendous cry. She

stumbled backwards. If Max had not been there to catch her, she would have tumbled to a cracked neck. But Max looped his arms under her and stopped her descent. Her skin felt pasty. Sweat broke out on her forehead. Her eyes bugged wide as she stared into something Max could not see.

And it ended. She closed her eyes and slumped in his arms.

Chapter 11

CRADLING IRENE IN HIS ARMS, Max hurried downstairs to the Reception Hall. He wanted to get her as far away from the attic stairs as possible. When he bent to rest her on the couch, Sandra pointed even further away — toward R.J. Reynolds' study.

"We don't want her in any of the rooms that have had activity," she said, her eyes shivering as much as her voice.

Drummond hovered over them the entire time. "She still breathing? She going to be okay?"

Max lifted the small woman and hustled toward the study. "I think she'll be fine."

"Suddenly you're a doctor. We should call for help."

"And say what? Hey Doc, could you please take a look at this patient who was attacked by a psychic connection?"

Drummond's eyes flared, but he withheld any further objection. Once Max rested Irene on the study couch, he stepped back with a relieved sigh. Sandra crouched next to the psychic and felt the woman's forehead.

"President Truman once slept on that couch," Max said, tapping his fingers against his legs.

Drummond raised an eyebrow. "Why are you telling us that? Again?"

"I don't know."

"Both of you, be quiet." Sandra leaned over Irene, pressing her forehead against the unconscious woman's forehead, and muttered soft words.

Max held back from asking questions, but it was not easy. Not when his wife attempted to cast a spell without a circle, without any candles, without anything but her voice and her willpower. If she succeeded, he knew he would be proud of her, but he also suspected he would fear her. No — not her, but the power within her. Maybe her concerns were valid. Maybe her studies in witchcraft could change her at the core level.

With several puttering coughs, Irene Beck awoke. She looked around disoriented as she tried to sit up. Max watched fascinated and horrified and unsure if Sandra's power had brought the woman back or if Irene had simply awoken on her own.

"Let me tell you something, dear," Drummond said. "You just gave all of us the biggest scare of the night."

Irene snickered. "Oh now, I highly doubt that."

"Really? Because from where I'm floating, I was certain you'd be joining me in the ghostly realm."

"Far from it. But that was certainly not a pleasant experience. I sure do hope I don't ever feel that way again."

Sandra said, "What happened exactly? None of us felt anything."

From her purse, Irene dug out a small white pill and popped it in her mouth. To the sudden frowns, she said, "It's a breath mint. I know what we're dealing with now. I've got a lot to tell you, and there ain't no reason for you to be suffering bad breath on top of everything else."

Max pulled the chair from behind R.J.'s desk and sat. More than any of the other furniture in the house, sitting in that chair — one of the earliest swivel chairs ever produced — Max felt the weight of history the house created.

It spoke to the deep ties within the family that once lived here. This furniture had belonged to them, had been used by them as the tools of life, not the property of a museum to be gawked at. For an instant, he could hear the running patter of the children as they played the ultimate game of hide and seek throughout the enormous house. He pictured Katherine dropping in this chair, exhausted from tending her ailing husband as he rested on the couch.

He wondered what those children had thought of their

father — a man who had died when they were so young. Did they connect to the little time they had with him? Or would it be some other male figure in their life that took the role? Max continued to do his best to take on that role for the Sandwich Boys. But would he be enough?

"This house," Max said, not intending to speak out loud.

"What about it?" Sandra said.

"Nothing. The place has this way of spiraling my thoughts into dark areas."

Irene snapped her fingers and pointed at Max. "Not the house. It's the spirit."

Drummond gently lowered to the floor. "Then there *is* a ghost here. Why can't I see it?"

"Not a ghost, a spirit. And not just any kind of spirit. As we walked up those stairs, I felt a furious presence that sucked the air right from my lungs. It thought that it had the upper-hand — I suppose, in most ways it did — but by attacking me, it also opened itself to being read. At least, a little. That's how I know that what we're dealing with is an inhuman spirit."

Her words dropped flat in the room, and though Max knew one of them had to ask the question, nobody wanted to do so. It was as if they had collectively agreed that by avoiding the question, they could avoid the answer, and thus, avoid the situation. It was magical thinking, of course, but the human mind often lied to itself, even if only for a moment.

That moment whisked by, and Max asked, "What exactly is an inhuman spirit?"

"That depends." Irene crossed her legs like a child — a manner both endearing and at odds with the words coming out of her mouth. "Obviously, we're talking about something that is not human and never was. As a spirit, it's possible that it may never have even lived in our world directly. A ghost is created when a human being dies and cannot move on for a myriad of reasons. But most spirits are already living on another plane, not the human corporeal world. You are not religious folk, if I recall."

"That's right," Sandra said.

"That's a shame. Religion often makes it easier to comprehend inhuman spirits. We can call them demons and all have a shared understanding of what we're talking about. I'm not saying they truly are creatures born in some hell, I wouldn't dare presume of Heaven and Hell, but there are good and evil places that exist beyond this world. That much cannot be too hard for you to understand, is it?"

"Once you've dealt with witches and ghosts, the rest is a little easier to swallow."

Irene chuckled. "I suppose so."

Max said, "Not being religious doesn't mean we can't comprehend the idea of a demon."

"But it's not really a demon," Irene said. "It's not some cloven-footed, spiky-tailed creature with a pitchfork. I only mentioned the idea of a demon because this particular spirit is of the evil persuasion. If you were thoroughly read in such things, then you could easily understand the nature of this evil."

Drummond nodded as if he had been studying at the seminary for most of his life. "Important thing for us to take away is that this thing is very dangerous. Not only is it violent, but we can't see it unless it wants to be seen. We can't even feel it, unless it wants to be felt. That about right?"

"Mostly, yes."

Max said, "Then how do we stop it?"

"That is the key question." She clutched her knees and inched forward as if about to reveal a damning secret. Whispering, she said, "I don't know exactly."

"What? After all of this, you can't help?"

"I'm saying that at this point in time, I don't know exactly because I don't know the precise nature of this inhuman spirit. I only got hit by it once. So, what we're going to do is return to that attic and face that beast. If this inhuman spirit is of a milder variety — which so far it has not displayed anything more to be in its power — then we should be able to convince it to leave of its own accord."

Max's shoulders relaxed. "Just ask it to leave? That'll work?"

"In some cases, yes."

"That's easy enough."

Irene lowered her head to look over the rims of her glasses. "No. It'll be the furthest thing from easy."

Chapter 12

ALTHOUGH IRENE SAID she could manage the attic right away, Drummond insisted that she rest up first. "You won't be any good to anybody if you're passing out again right when we step in that place," he said, making no effort to hide the concern from his face.

After a few half-hearted refusals, she agreed — but only if Drummond remained by her side. Max thought that had been Drummond's intent all along. Regardless of the way the old ghost wanted to play the situation, the end result remained the same — Max and Sandra left the study to give the ghost and the psychic some privacy.

Sandra went off to retrieve her bag, and Max walked around the library. With any luck, this entity felt much like Drummond when it came to libraries. If not, then no room in the house was safe.

Grinning at the thought, Max meandered around the room. He avoided looking at the paintings — no need to take unnecessary risks — and let his attention rove from the floral upholstery to the beautifully carved tables to the cigarette box with an ivory insert. In the center of this insert, surrounded by a circle, a warrior on a horse trampled his enemy. All around this central image, cherubic faces, cornucopias, and lions in mid-roar had been carved.

Max had to bring his head close to the box in order to see the full details. The warrior appeared to be bald except for a long, flowing tail off the top of his head like a classical depiction of a djinn. Max shuddered and stepped away. With all the strange imagery he had witnessed throughout the house, he marveled that the place had not been haunted before this.

From down the hall, Drummond's voice lifted. Max crossed to the doorway and listened. He could not make out the words exchanged, but the tones spoke to an intimacy he had not realized the couple had achieved. He knew that they had become infatuated with each other — that much was obvious — but Max never saw Drummond as a man driven by such things. The ghost talked like he had those thoughts, but Max assumed it was either residual behavior from his days living or simply talk. At least, when it came to living, breathing, human beings. Drummond spoke of time spent with other ghosts, but a human?

Stranger, still, Irene Beck embraced the relationship, too. Max could comprehend why a ghost might seek out human contact of this sort — a chance to feel human again, even if only an elusive idea — but what could Irene get out of this?

"Eavesdropping?" Sandra said as she entered the library carrying her bag.

Max reddened before crossing his arms and plopping down on the couch. "I worry for Drummond. Don't want him getting his heart broken. He suffers enough as a ghost."

"I know. But he might get some joy out of the overall experience, too."

"If you start quoting that it's better to have loved and lost —"

"He's a big boy. Trust that he knows what he wants and needs."

Max chuckled. "Look at me. I'm now acting parental to a ghost."

"Maybe this'll help," she said, producing Drummond's whiskey flask from her bag.

"Okay, now I'm convinced you've put a spell on that bag. When did you swipe this?"

Beaming, Sandra said, "While you dropped off the boys."

"You said you went out to get some things we needed to last the night. I didn't think you meant this."

"I figured if this all turned out to be nothing or something minor, we could spend the rest of the night just us two. So, I swung by the office and grabbed it. Drummond wasn't around or I would have asked for his permission. I didn't think we'd need this for anything but pleasure, yet here we are."

Max tipped back a swig from the flask. "Here we are, indeed. So, what do you think about Drummond? His whole story about his father and all?"

"My gut reaction — I was glad to hear it. Made me happy to know that he was your partner whenever you were working a case without me."

"Didn't you hear him? He thinks of us as far more than partners. He called us *family*."

"After all that we've been through with him, wouldn't you call him family, too?"

"Well, yeah, but ... I mean ... it's not like I ever planned for a ghost to be my partner ... let alone a member of my family."

After tipping back the flask herself, Sandra screwed on the top and returned it to her bag. She squeezed Max's knee, leaned over, and kissed his cheek. "Sometimes you're adorable when you're confused about the obvious."

"Great. Mocking me again, and I don't even understand why."

"Hon, you need to accept that the life we're living is far removed from the life we expected to live. It's okay. We never planned to have kids. We didn't want them. We never planned to have this crazy life working cases against witches and ghosts and now, inhuman spirits. But that's okay, too. If life had come out the way we predicted or planned, it would not have been much of a life. Don't you know by now that it's the unexpected twists — both good and bad — that make your life worth living? You may not appreciate it at the time, but at the end, when you're looking back, you realize how important those twists were. It's the very essence of what we need it to be."

"How can you say that?" Max tried not to be angry. He wasn't, he told himself. He didn't feel angry. Yet these thoughts boiled in him at times. The hotter they boiled, the more he heard his voice snap out. All he could think — it was the house. No, not the house — the inhuman spirit in the house.

Sandra had said that it fed off negative energy. Maybe it had a way of manipulating people into creating the energy it needed.

Taking a deep breath, working at remaining calm, he said, "I can't even get you to agree that we've succeeded in building our family, yet you want me to accept all the unplanned and sometimes bad things that happen in our life are the most important parts. That doesn't make any sense."

She took his hand and kissed his knuckles. "It's not that I don't agree with the idea that we've succeeded in making a family. We have. But it's not perfect. It never will be. And that's okay. It supposed to be that way. That's what I'm trying to get you to understand. There is no finish line to having a family. It's not a moment of perfection that you can achieve. It's more like an accumulation of moments, a shared history between people, a trusted and bonding love. It is all those mistakes and bad moments balled up with the good, all shared between a group of people. That's a family, and that's what we have. With you and me, with the Sandwich Boys, with Drummond, and even with your mother."

Max closed his eyes and rested against the back of the couch. "That's a lot to think about."

He listened to the soft laugh of his wife. She said, "Lucky for you, your family doesn't require you to understand it all tonight."

Easy enough to be said, but Max knew he would not let these thoughts leave. He might as well be researching the idea because when his mind latched onto something like that, it refused to let go until he found the information he sought. It was like having a bloodhound for a brain, and while he normally took pride in that fact, this night, he wished he could let it all go.

"Do you think it's too late for our boys?" he asked. "I'm not looking for a pat on the back and I'm not fishing for any kind of complement. But I wonder if the true value of a parent is in the beginning, in the early stages of a child's life. PB and J are not that far away from being adults."

"Far enough."

"They're teenagers. Just starting, but you get my point, right?"

"I do. And if you would pay more attention to their actual reactions, instead of your own worries, you might see how much they love having us as their parents. They know the absence they had. They know what it's like to have a father walk out on them. As long as you keep showing up, they will always appreciate it, and your presence will have a greater impact upon them than you'll ever realize."

"Just to be clear — I have no intention of running out on you."

Sandra placed her arm across his waist. "Well then, it's good one of us is committed to staying."

She said the words so calm and loving that it took him a moment to realize what she had actually said. Then he laughed. "You better watch it with that kind of humor. The wrong person hears that, and all the hard work we've done to become official parents will be undone."

"Then it's a good thing we're in an empty house."

Drummond's head entered through the wall. "Irene's back on her feet. You both ready to get to work?"

Max and Sandra lifted their heads and stared at Drummond. Both of them broke into uproarious laughter.

Chapter 13

DRUMMOND DRIFTED IN FRONT OF IRENE like a bodyguard keeping the path ahead clear. Max and Sandra followed up to the second floor balcony. Once at the base of the next flight of stairs, the ones leading to the attic, everybody paused.

At first, nobody spoke. Nobody wanted to admit that they all feared what might come. That fear painted the air with a foul odor. A foulness roiling their stomachs.

With the kindness of a loving grandmother, Irene finally broke the silence. "It's going to be okay. I wasn't ready for what we faced before. But now, I know my enemy."

Sandra said, "If you would like, I would be happy to cast a spell that will offer you some protection. It may not be much, but a little bit of a shield is better than nothing."

Irene reached up to pat Sandra's shoulder. "So kind of you, but not necessary. Faith is what's needed here. I may not always show it, but I have a deep and strong appreciation for the Lord." She looked off to the sky and scrunched her brow. "Not so much for the church, but then, organized religion has never been my thing. The faith I hold, however, is real enough to protect me."

"I'm sorry," Max said, "and I'm not trying to be a jerk, but we've faced a lot of strange things before this, and faith has never been enough to protect us from anything."

"Well now, child, you're talking about puttin' lipstick on a pig, aren't you? You want faith to protect you, but you don't have any. You're an atheist. Any spirit — inhuman or not — is going to see through false faith. But mine will shine like a bright, glorious light. It's not the false belief in doctrine or words written by some patriarchy trying to twist the world into their view — no, no. My faith is a simple one, and that's what makes it so strong. I have faith that the Lord exists. That He sees all and that He will protect me, should I need protecting."

Max did not like anything she had to say. Not so much because of the religious aspect but rather the failures of logic. If the Lord did exist, and if the Lord was going to protect her, then why did she get attacked in the first place? At the same time, he had to admit that he had seen ghosts and witches react to true faith before. Plus, the very idea of the word *faith* was to believe in something unquestioningly — even in the face of defying logic. On top of all that, Max recognized that, at the very least, Irene's faith would give her the courage needed in order to climb the stairs.

Max, however, did not need faith. He had Sandra, and he had Drummond. They gave him all the courage he required. They always did.

Irene faced the stairs, and like a brave warrior heading off to battle, she marched up. Drummond still maintained the lead, but Max got the sense that should the ghost stop, Irene would have stomped right through him. Sandra went next, and Max trudged up as the caboose.

At the halfway point, they all hesitated. But when nothing attacked Irene or any of the others, they continued on their way.

Max tried not to hold any expectations as he entered the attic. Still, it was not what he expected. On the surface, the attic had been finished off with walls and ceiling as well as a comfortable, carpeted floor. According to the information he had on hand, the attic had originally been simply that — an attic used for the storage of Katherine's many fine dresses and clothing, the toys the children had outgrown, and other items too precious to dispose of but not necessary to daily life. In 1973, Nancy Reynolds saw to the conversion of the attic into a place that showed off three generations of the family's belongings. More than any part of the house, the attic felt like a museum. Fine dresses from the 1920s were displayed on mannequins while a shelf near the ceiling exhibited numerous women's shoes. Hats, a sewing machine, toy cars, baby dresses, jacks and balls, and plenty more all had their place in this miniature set up.

Where the rest of the house presented each room either exactly as it had been or as close as the curators could reproduce, the place still felt vibrant with life. Take down the velvet ropes and signs preventing people from using the furniture, and it would not be difficult to believe somebody had chosen to live on this estate — someone who enjoyed antique furniture and furnishings. But the attic — here time truly froze. Here the memories and artifacts of lives long gone had been resurrected and put on display.

As odd and disjointed as this room felt when compared to the rest of the house, it did not account for the anxiety Max felt coursing through his veins. Obviously, facing an inhuman spirit held the bulk of that honor. But he knew where the other small percentage came from.

Growing up, there was a walk-in closet next to the door to his mother's room. This closet served much the same purpose as the Reynolda House attic — it stored the forgotten clothing, the outgrown toys, the knickknacks and unwanted doodads that Max's mother refused to discard but had no use for. It also happened to be the place she hid his Christmas gifts, his birthday gifts, or any other special item she needed to keep from his young eyes. As a result, Max knew that whenever a special occasion approached, entering the walk-in closet without permission — and getting caught — would bring a heavy penalty. His mother never outright said that, but this unspoken rule had been made clear.

Standing in the Reynolda House attic left Max feeling as if he had violated one of those rules. "Small suggestion," he said, disliking the flat sound of his voice in this tiny room. "Let's get this over with as quick as possible."

Drummond said, "I'm inclined to agree. The longer we're here, the more opportunities this inhuman thing has to take another swipe at Irene."

"Stop that," Irene said. "This is not a time for chivalry. I need everyone's confidence and bravery. I need you to dig down and find the courage you have that has brought you this far in your life. And if you have it for anything, your faith."

Sandra inched closer to Max, and he laced his fingers in hers. Without a specific word spoken between the group, they knew the time had come. Irene stepped forward and stopped in the center of the room. It had a low ceiling which coupled with the tension bouncing between them all, made this short woman appear taller, stronger.

"If after everything I have said," Irene began, "you still have not found anything to believe in, anything to have faith in, then believe in me. I am ready for this."

She closed her eyes and inhaled, raising her hands up to her shoulders. When she exhaled, she pressed her hands down as if pushing the air out of her body. Three times she repeated this motion before settling into a calm, open eyed, presence of being. She looked ahead as if meditating, only her awareness of the moment had not shifted away.

With a voice that could have carried throughout the entire estate, Irene said, "Spirit in this house, I call upon you to leave this premises. I do not wish any harm to come to you, but you are not welcome here. You are not welcome in this world. You do not belong here."

The walls banged like a rumble of thunder.

Irene continued, "You do not belong here, and you should never have come. I call upon you to listen and heed what I say. For I am here with the Lord's protection. The Lord is with me, and the Lord shall see me through my dealings with you."

The thunderous walls grew louder. Sandra's fingers tightened on Max's hand. He wanted to whisper some assurances to her — more for his own comfort than hers — but he feared breaking Irene's concentration.

"This house does not belong to you," Irene went on. "This is not your territory. You do not belong here."

Two mannequins toppled to the floor. Max could feel the vibrations through his feet. Photographs on the walls bounced while small toys on a table jittered. The rattling noise of jewelry and shoes and belt buckles added to the growing discord.

In a voice that somehow rose above the spirit's storming anger, Irene said, "Obey me. Hear me. This house does not belong to you and never has. The Lord is with me, and in his name, I command you to leave at once."

Long cracks snaked across the ceiling. Bits of drywall fell to the floor. And then — it stopped.

For one foolish second, Max grinned. The thought that little Irene Beck had saved them all brought a flicker of joy into his chest.

Until a heavy thick voice rolled up from the floor and through the walls and down from the ceiling. "No."

Irene stumbled back as if struck. Drummond soared across to her side.

In the center of the room, right where Irene had stood seconds before, a swirling orb of purplish light formed. It fluttered bright like a strobe at a nightclub. Yet despite the bizarre nature of this thing, despite the maddening existence of it, all eyes turned toward Drummond. The light from the orb reflected against his face and body as if he was a solid object. As if he was not a ghost.

Glancing down at his hands, Drummond frowned. "What the heck is this?"

Chapter 14

IRENE SNAPPED HER FINGERS. "Stop gawking at Marshall, and everyone make a circle around this thing."

Max took a position opposite Irene with Drummond to his left and Sandra to his right. Only a few seconds in the presence of this orb and he had no doubt that Sandra had been correct — this thing fed off negativity. The anger, the frustration, the evil blistering from that thing hit Max like a Southern summer wall of heat.

He glanced at Sandra. She offered a short nod and it sent comfort throughout him. Not enough to soothe his hammering heart, not enough to break down the thicket of knotty fear tying up his muscles and veins, but enough to provide the strength to continue. He lacked religious faith, but he believed in Sandra.

"Spirit in this house," Irene said, "I stand before you with the Lord as my shepherd. I lead this concert of good and courageous people, and we demand that you leave this house."

The orb continued to flicker its light — at times a dark purple, at times so bright it blinded like staring at the sun. But Max noticed that he could hear nothing beyond a static crackle. Perhaps the energy required to form this orb left the inhuman spirit incapable of shaking the walls and quaking the floor. While he had no desire for the spirit to return to its previous state of being, he found the flickering light and the deadened sound in the attic to be more unnerving.

"We command you to leave. Leave this house at once and never return." Irene's voice no longer carried far. She sounded like a mere human instead of a force that could cover all the acres of the estate by sheer will.

Behind her, shadows danced along the walls — strange purplish images brought on by mannequins and stuffed animals. They shifted with the changes in the light, sometimes laughing, sometimes scolding, sometimes barking mad. Max watched this shadow puppet show, and his mind kept searching for the story until he reminded himself that he had to focus on the task at hand.

It's the spirit playing with your head, he told himself. *Come on, Max. Hold onto your strength.*

"What are you trying to do?" Sandra whispered.

Max resisted the urge to shush her. Especially after he saw that Irene had gestured to Sandra, opening up the floor for her input. The question had not been at him but at the spirit. Swallowing back a tinge of jealousy, Max turned his attention entirely on the psychic. Now that the question had been asked, he wanted to hear the answer.

When nothing came, Irene said, "We can't know for sure. One way or another, though, my guess is that it's trying to create as much fear and anger as it can. Don't look for an inhuman spirit to think like a human. But like any being — it can get hungry."

Max raised his hand. "Is it okay to talk now?"

"No. This is not for you. Not unless you know the answer to your wife's question."

Max had a witty reply — at least, he thought of it as witty — but he clamped his mouth shut. She was wrong, of course. If Sandra could talk, then Max could contribute just as much or as little as the rest of them. In fact, the history of the Porter Agency had proven on almost every occasion that his contributions to the team were vital. While he lacked Sandra's ability to see all ghosts and her ability to tap into witchcraft, that did not make him useless. Though Drummond had the ability to pass through walls and go to the Other, that did not make Max an unintended appendage to the team. Without him, they would never know what to go looking for. He did the research. He connected the dots. He knew how to dig up the key pieces of information that others couldn't find. For crying out loud, Sandra referred to his research ability as his superpower. No matter what Irene thought, Max knew that wasn't condescension. Sandra believed it. And so did he.

"You okay?" Drummond said as softly as possible.

Max waved him off, but the interruption brought his attention to the thoughts he had been spiraling with — negative thoughts. He looked straight at the orb. He felt watched by it. No — more than that. He felt observed. That orb stared into him as if it wore a lab coat and held a clipboard. It unraveled whatever defenses Max had as it attempted to worm its way into him. To feed.

"Are we just going to stand here and let this thing have its way?" Max heard the snap in his voice. Indeed, everybody heard it.

Irene put out her hands. "Breathe. Calm yourself. Find your faith again."

Max gazed at Sandra. He could smell her — a mixture of her perfume, her soap, and her skin like lemongrass and roses. She looked back at him, and he marveled at how incredible her eyes could make him feel. Without a word, she had the ability to melt away the world around them. She lifted him into the air, and they could float to another town, another country, another planet, — heck, another plane of existence. In her arms, he felt the surety that all the demons of the world would be repelled. Nothing could pierce the love between them.

Yet those were the notions of a twenty-year-old falling in love. They were not kids anymore. They were responsible for kids now. They could not simply snuggle under the covers in a hotel room for the weekend, letting their body heat ignite and reignite their passions, pushing the world and all its problems away, leaving them tied together in their own private bubble. That option no longer existed for them. Because of this.

His focus shifted back to the orb.

An inhuman spirit. A ghost detective. A psychic. Witches and magic and curses. All of it had warped his life into this unruly mass.

He ground his teeth and clenched his fists. The orb flickered faster, brighter.

"Fight, partner," Drummond said.

With an edge of panic creeping into her voice, Irene said, "Spirit in this house, unwelcome visitor, you've refused to leave, that is clear. If you won't go, then why do you stay? What do you want?"

The air shifted. It felt colder, thicker, fraught with menace. Max set his right foot back and lowered his center of gravity — a martial arts fighting stance. He did not think he could battle this glowing orb of hate. He did not think about it at all. His body simply moved — preparing for whatever response came to Irene's question.

But nothing happened.

It felt like a minute, possibly more, still nothing happened.

Irene cleared her throat. "This is your only chance. Answer me. Tell me why you are here, what you want, and maybe we can help you. But if you continue to stand in our way and terrorize those who visit this dwelling, then I will have to perform a formal cleaning of the house. I will see you banished far away from here. Look into me, and you will feel my conviction. My faith in the Lord is strong, and you will fall to me."

While Max did not doubt the depth of Irene's faith, he wondered if she truly possessed the power she claimed to have. If a bluff, she impressed him greatly. If true, she frightened him as well.

"So be it," she said. "We'll have to do this the hard way."

The orb brightened. Like stones grating against each other, it spoke. "A body. A soul."

Max's fingers rolled into tight fists. His body wanted to throw that punch even as his mind wondered where such a punch could be landed.

"A body. A soul." The words ground so hard against each other that everyone leaned forward to try to decipher their meaning.

Irene took three small steps closer. "If what you mean to say is —"

The orb shimmered. Its crackling energy became a sharp sizzle as it flattened into a javelin shape. Then it shot forward, heading right towards Irene.

Drummond didn't have time to finish shouting her name. The orb slammed against her chest, but instead of cutting through her, its bright energy splayed off into several directions. She stumbled back but remained standing.

She even chuckled — not with humor but with conviction. "My faith protects me. My Lord protects me, and in the name of that faith, in the name of my Lord, I command you to leave this house."

The javelin shaped energy reformed and took on Max as its new target. What should have happened in an instant, however, slowed for Max as his hyper-focused mind worked in concert with his handful of years training. He remembered to breathe. When he exhaled, he saw the javelin headed straight for his heart. His body performed well-rehearsed moves.

Stepping with his left foot, he pivoted to the side. A simple maneuver that removed him from the javelin's path. Normally, he would follow up with a strike to the body as his enemy soared by, but in this case, he did not want to touch that thing at all.

A half second later, the inhuman spirit splashed against the wall, its energy spreading out and reforming to find a new target. Max had no doubt where it would go next — Sandra.

He lunged across the room and wrapped his arms around her, presenting his back to the javelin as it crashed into them. He felt the pressure, it pushed him deeper against Sandra. He yelled as he braced for the pain — but it did not happen. The two had held their ground. Irene had been right. Their faith in one another protected them.

Max glanced over his shoulder at Drummond — the next obvious target. But the spirit shot its javelin body through the floor and disappeared. Max held Sandra tight, waiting for the next attack. After a moment, Irene waved them all to circle up.

Stepping back, Max said, "Huh. I guess it doesn't like ghosts."

Drummond winked. "We're not as tasty as you'd think. Besides, it wasn't going to be able to hit me. I wouldn't have even needed to block it, just let it go right through to the other side of me."

Still holding onto Max, Sandra said, "At least everybody's okay. The question now is —"

Four enormous arms erupted out of the floor. Though the same odd purple color, they lacked the solidity of the orb or the javelin. With long, clawed fingernails on thick hands, these arms reached straight up into the air. Max saw right through them. The spirit had changed itself. It was a pale purple now — ghostly pale.

Drummond's eyes widened as he registered the difference, too. The arms bent towards him, the hands grabbed hold, and the claws dug in.

Max reached out. "Drummond!" But he didn't know what to do, what to say. He stared at his ghost partner — ineffectual and helpless.

Drummond pushed at the arms, yanked them off, shoved them aside, but they kept coming back. More emerged from the carpeted floor. Some grew out of the arms already attacking him.

Irene cried out. "Leave this house. I command you."

While fighting off the arms, Drummond pressed towards Max and Sandra. He reached out for them, his eyes peering between two claws that clutched his face. Max wanted to do something, anything. He felt the cold of the ghost world pushing up to him but had no idea how to help.

Drummond continued to struggle until three more arms shot up, latched onto his shoulders, and dragged him down with ferocious effort. Right through the floor.

In an instant, all grew quiet. The chill of ghostly bodies left the room.

Irene dropped to her knees. Her body wracked with sobs. Sandra covered her mouth in shock. Part of Max wanted to put his arm around his wife. Part of him wanted to say something comforting to Irene. But most of him could only stare at the floor and wonder — had he just lost his closest friend?

"Help!" Drummond's voice sounded distant through the floor. Irene put her hand on the carpet, digging into the fibers as if she could pull Drummond back into the room. Sandra wiped the tears from her eyes. But Max's head perked up.

"Did you hear that?"

"Of course," Irene said. "We all heard him. Calling from beyond."

"Not from beyond. I don't hear things from some otherworld beyond. That's your realm. I hear Drummond but only when he's here with me. Which means — he's still here. And if it dragged him through the floor ..."

Max whirled toward the stairs and bolted out of the attic.

Chapter 15

HE TORE DOWN THE STAIRS, skipping the last three with a leap. He dashed out to the balcony and smashed into the railing. His heart rushed up to his neck as his legs lifted and he angled over the edge, staring at the drop to the main floor of the Reception Hall. As the railing dug into his side, he saw Drummond — waist high in the floor, scrabbling with his fingers to find purchase on something that would allow him to pull free. And those hands — those clawed hands cuffed around his wrists, gripping his throat, dragging him deeper down through the wood.

"Hold on," Max said, rolling back to his feet. He sprinted to the main stairwell and jumped halfway down. When he hit the stairs again, he lost his footing and slid all the way to the bottom. Each step slammed into his back promising a purple-black row of bruises along his spine. When he hit the end, he popped to his feet and jetted for Drummond.

Whatever pain his fall had produced, he felt none of it. Not yet. He didn't have time for pain.

Drummond punched at the arms beneath the floor. Max looked for anything that he could use to fish Drummond in. Something for the ghost to grab hold of. But his partner sank fast.

By the fireplace, Max spotted an iron poker. He picked it up but hesitated. He recalled reading somewhere that pure iron would hurt a ghost much like pure salt.

"Max," Drummond said, his voice muted.

Max spun around — no Drummond. But he did catch the last of the man's hat as it sucked into the wood.

Dashing across to the secondary stairwell that led to the

basement, Max dodged the furniture, his flashlight jittering in his shaking hands. When he reached the stairs, narrow and dark, his flashlight did little to save him from another fall. If not for the walls brushing his shoulders, he would have plunged into the darkness and probably to his death. But as he lost his balance, he simply pressed his hands out on either side to stop his momentum.

When he reached the bottom, he found a finished basement with a hard, black-rubber tile floor. A billiard table took up the space of one section, and signs pointed to a bowling alley, shooting gallery, and ping-pong tables. But Drummond's voice led Max down a winding hall and into a room designed to mimic a 1930s-style bar. Mirrors lined the curved walls. Bright red upholstery shined, reflected in the chrome surfaces of circular cocktail tables. Very Art Deco. And in the middle of the dark floor, Drummond fought the numerous purple clawed hands.

Though the orb had disappeared, its flickering light rippled from beneath Drummond. This was it. Max could tell — this was the hole that would swallow Drummond for good.

The bright lights bounced off the mirrors and the chrome surfaces creating a dazzling, disorienting display as if plum wine splashed in the air. Max needed something to help his partner — something not made of iron, or metal since he didn't know how far that concept went. Wood. That might work.

Max rushed back to the billiard room. From the wall, he grabbed a pool cue and raced to Drummond. "Grab onto this."

Drummond reached out, willed his body to take solid form, and endure the pain of touching the corporeal world as his hands latched around the end of the pool cue.

Max leaned back like the anchor in a tug-of-war. His muscles burned, and the abuse his back had taken flared up. Grunting, wincing, he dug his feet in and tried to push back another inch. Another one. Every little bit pulling Drummond out of that nightmare hole.

Salty sweat seeped into Max's mouth. A wretched stink like rotten eggs burped up from the hole in the floor. Drummond managed to get his other hand free and clasped the pool cue immediately. The claws digging into him tore at his shirt.

He screamed.

Max had no idea if the clothes a ghost wore were simply clothes or if they were part of his ghostly being, but one thing proved true enough — it all hurt. He had never seen such anguish on Drummond's face before. Anguish and doubt. Drummond didn't think he was going to make it.

"Don't give up," Max said.

A large, muscular arm spewed from the floor. It grew long and limber, and Max watched it tower behind Drummond. He thought with certainty that this hand would clamp onto Drummond's head and shoved the ghost down. But Max was wrong.

The hand did come down, but not upon Drummond. It smashed through the pool cue, severing the stick in two. Wood splintered off as Drummond and Max fell away from each other. Max's head banged against one of the cocktail tables. The numerous arms around Drummond wrenched him all the way down to his chest.

"No!" Max scuttled across the floor. He thrust out his hand. "Grab me."

Drummond clinched hands with Max. Razors of ice sliced through Max's palm, up his arm, and straight to the bone. He swore, he wailed, his throat scratching at the volume forced out of him. Drummond bellowed his own wracking pain.

Trying to contract his muscles, Max worked to haul Drummond closer. But the cold numbed his body at the same time as it burned him in ice-drenched fire. He could barely think let alone force his body to perform an action.

Through his narrowed eyes, Max saw Drummond, saw the look on his face, saw the loss in his eyes. The ghost knew it, and so did Max. There were too many arms to fight against. They didn't have the strength between them. Not when touching each other caused such intense agony.

Sounding too much like an old man, Drummond said, "I won't stop fighting."

He let go of Max's hand.

Max flopped onto his back and listened to Drummond's cries die into silence. Warm blood flowed through his veins causing the most excruciating pins and needles he had ever experienced. Forcing his body to sit up, he stared at the empty floor as he massaged his arm.

Sandra and Irene rushed in. They looked around, looked at Max, trying to understand the situation. Max lifted his head toward both of them.

A tear streaked down to his chin. "He's gone."

Chapter 16

FURTHER DOWN FROM THE BAR, the hallway took a sharp left and ended with another highlight of Reynolda House — the indoor pool. Encased in textured glass like a greenhouse, the pool provided a comfortable climate for swimming at all times of the year — even with winter nipping at the break of autumn. Max, Sandra, and Irene sat on the patio furniture surrounding the pool. No one could speak.

At times, Sandra rubbed Max's back or leaned her head on his shoulder. At times, he did the same for her. There were even moments when the two of them comforted Irene with a nod or a grim smile. They all felt the loss.

But after a few minutes, Max jumped to his feet and paced a circle around the pool. "This isn't over. We're going to get him back."

Sandra said, "Of course, we will. Tomorrow, we can —"

"No. We start now." Max rolled his lips in and thought.

Irene motioned as if she was going to interrupt him, but Sandra put a stop to that. Like a voice in the distance, she said, "Let him think."

Yeah. Let me think.

It sounded good, but his thoughts did not lead anywhere useful. He kept seeing the desperation on Drummond's face. He saw the pain and the impending loss in the way Drummond accepted his fate. All because of that inhuman spirit.

And thinking of the inhuman spirit brought to mind the images it had dropped into Max — images of his father with a malicious and terrifying grin. Images of blood and death.

Max stopped mid-step. "Why Drummond? This thing has focused on me since we got here. It threw me across the room, it gave me that horrible experience in the Lake Porch. Yet in the attic, it tried once to attack Irene and once to strike at us, but then it gave up. It went right after Drummond. Why?"

He paused, waited, and realized they thought he had asked rhetorically. He gestured for an answer. He needed an answer. This wasn't a normal case where he could ponder the situation and let his thoughts lead him to deeper research. He didn't have uninterrupted hours upon hours to get lost in the rabbit holes of books and the internet to find one little nugget that would glue it all together. He only had his researching intuition — the thing that led him to ask questions.

Finally, Sandra said, "Perhaps the inhuman spirit wants to use Drummond as a bargaining chip."

Irene jumped to her feet. With her mascara running deep rivulets down her face, she looked both crazed and fierce. "An inhuman spirit does not bargain. It wants what it wants and this one does not appear to be willing to stop until it gets when it came for."

"Which is not Drummond," Max said, stabbing his finger in the air as if pointing at the answer.

"Not if we believe what it said to us — and I do believe it. When I asked the spirit what it wanted, it said quite clearly that it needed a body and a soul. In other words, it wants to possess someone so it can walk freely in our world. It wants to possess that person completely, down to the soul, so that it cannot be removed from the world without ripping apart the possessed person. It wants the soul as insurance."

Sandra said, "Oh, is that all?"

"It's not that uncommon."

"Really? Because we've never seen one of these inhuman spirits before."

"I mean to say that yes, it's rare for an inhuman spirit to touch our plane of existence, to come close enough that we have problems like this; however, when these instances do happen, it's fairly common for the inhuman spirit to want to possess somebody. I had hoped that this would've been different. But I guess not."

Max resumed his pacing. "This brings me back to the first question — why Drummond? If this spirit wants a body and a soul, of what use is a ghost?"

"None, in regard to its ultimate goal. Still, if I had to hazard a guess, and I suppose I do, I would say this spirit hopes to siphon power off of Drummond, off of his ghostly essence, until it finds an opportunity to try for a more permanent solution again."

"Again? So, all those attacks on me before were its attempt to possess me?"

"More likely, the spirit tried to send you into a negative spiral so it could feed off that energy. Get stronger. Strong enough to possess you. But in the attic, it could no longer get that source of food. You and Sandra together were able to repel its attack. My faith in the Lord protected me. But Drummond is a ghost. Faith does not protect the dead."

Sandra said, "Once it could no longer get a human, it took what it hoped would be an easy path. Grab Drummond, and it's now feeding off his energy."

"That's right," Irene said. She turned to Sandra. "You should understand that this thing will get more than enough energy from Drummond. He's a strong ghost. His time with you has filled him with a sense of life that he hasn't had since the day he died."

"You could feel that?"

"No, sweetie, he told me. We're friends. I don't need to read him like a client."

Max said, "Then we've got to stop this thing. We've got to save Drummond before it drains him dry."

Sandra gazed upon him with such pride, that he could not help but swell a little in the chest. When she stood, however, her brow knitted into inquisitive concentration — he'd seen that look many times whenever she studied witchcraft. He waited. A question would be coming soon, one he had not considered, and one he expected would help them greatly. Sandra did not disappoint.

Facing Irene, Sandra said, "How does something like this

inhuman spirit even start?"

Max wanted to kiss her. She was absolutely right. They needed to understand the foundation of the problem before they could unravel a real solution.

"Two ways, usually," Irene said, scooting forward to set her feet on the floor. "Sometimes, it happens by accident. Same way they get this hunger to possess another and be in our world. Within their plane of existence, they somehow skim the surface of ours."

"And the second way?"

"That's a more insidious situation. If it is indeed the second way, and there are no other ways I know of to consider, well, it means that somebody must've called for it. On purpose."

"Like with a summoning spell?"

"It can be done that way. Difficult witchcraft, but possible. However, y'all said you'd searched this place and found no evidence of witchcraft."

"That's right."

"A spell like that would require close proximity. And the summoned creature would be bound to the spell. There's nothing like that around here."

Max's synapses started firing links between his thoughts. Not enough to form a conclusive idea in his head, but enough that he felt it — a foreboding in his chest that punctured his pride with worry. "If not by witchcraft, how else would somebody go about calling this inhuman spirit?"

Irene looked away. She suddenly discovered the need to freshen her face. Gazing in the mirror of a compact that she pulled from her purse, she wiped clean her mascara and touched up whatever blemishes she found. All the while, she spoke with enough trepidation to chill Max's skin. "There are other spells — ceremonies, really. Not witchcraft. It doesn't use the standard symbols and procedures of witchcraft. As a result, these ceremonies produce widely varied and highly unstable results. But some people believe that it is possible to call upon an inhuman spirit and strike a deal. In many religions, they consider it a deal with the devil, a crossroads deal, an unholy bargain. What you call it depends on where you come from, but the idea is the same."

"You're saying that somebody summoned this inhuman spirit to make a deal for fortune and fame?"

"Could be for anything a person imagines."

Nodding as his brain connected more ideas, Max said, "I take it that in exchange for whatever this person wanted, they'd have to provide a soul."

"In most belief systems, people are taught that you have to give up your own soul for the deal. But that's a bending of the truth intended to caution them away from this stupid and dangerous act. The full truth is that the inhuman spirit doesn't care where the soul comes from."

Sandra said, "It also wants a body, right?"

"Most certainly."

Max's eyes widened as the implications mounted. His face tightened, and he threw several wild punches into the air. "We were set up. We were intended to be the sacrifice for this inhuman spirit all along."

"Offering," Sandra said, her own muscles contracting as she clutched her hands together.

"Only one person put us here. That bastard, Mr. Carroll. He didn't even care which of us got destroyed. He must've figured that the inhuman spirit would take down one of us and the other would simply think it was a case gone bad."

Irene put away her compact and stood. "More than likely. Now that we know, what do we do about it?"

As Max spoke, he stormed toward the exit of the pool. "We go to Mr. Carroll's office. That man has to answer a lot of questions."

Chapter 17

MARCHING BACK UPSTAIRS, through the halls of the house, into the lobby, and down the stairs toward the administrative offices, Max felt energy surging through him — strong, positive energy. He needed to do something that moved them forward toward Drummond, and now he gained a chance. He had a lead, and he wasn't going to waste it.

When they reached Mr. Carroll's door, Max turned the knob. Locked. He pulled out the master key Mr. Carroll had provided, but it would not fit. Max stared at the unmoving handle, and for a moment, he had no idea what to do. In the past, he would ask his partner to slip through the wall, endure the short burst of pain required to touch the knob, and unlock the door from the inside. But he didn't have a ghost partner anymore. At least, not one who could help him right now.

"I'm still not very good at picking locks," he said.

Sandra shrugged. "Don't look at me. Unless you want me to try creating a lock-picking spell on the fly."

"Step aside," Irene said.

Max raised his eyebrows. "You know how to pick a lock?"

"Well, bless your heart. I'm a Southern gal through and through. My great-granddaddy used to run moonshine in and out of Winston-Salem. Trust me — I got all kinds of skills you wouldn't even dream of."

From her purse, Irene pulled out a hairpin and a safety pin. "Now, I should warn you, I haven't done this in ages. I'll be a little rusty."

Max and Sandra leaned against the opposite wall and waited. With the little clicks of Irene's work and the huffing grunts of her concentration as their backdrop, Sandra brought her head close to Max and said, "How are you doing?"

"Terrible. But you're hurting, too. Even Irene is. Drummond means so much to all of us."

"But he's been your partner the longest. If we're going to succeed at getting him back, we need your mind working at full strength. It's going to be hard for you to maintain the kind of focus necessary when Drummond is in such serious trouble."

"I'll be fine. I've been able to keep my wits about me when you've been in trouble or the boys or any number of other terrible situations — including situations putting my own life at risk. This is no different."

"Every time is different. Not only because the particulars are different, but because they happen at a different point in your life. You were different today than you were a few years ago. The things that matter to you now may not have even been on your radar a few years back when we started all this."

"What are you trying to say?"

"You need to be careful. When you're passionate about something, sometimes you rush in without thinking. Sometimes you jump to conclusions that don't have facts supporting them. If you end up doing something like that and it results in us losing Drummond forever, it'll destroy you. And us."

With a single clap of her hands — one too reminiscent of Drummond — Irene opened the door to Mr. Carroll's office. "It really is like riding a bike."

They entered, and Max's first impression could be summed up with one word — *witch.* The small office had a basic, metal desk and a single chair behind it. If another chair existed in that room, Max could not see it from all the clutter filling every available space. Books double-lined the shelves, stacks of papers piled on the floor, and large binders filled with reports, inventories, and all manner of paperwork had been strewn about. There were other items, too — things more personal to Mr. Carroll and less to do with the running of Reynolda House. Toy figurines of superheroes stood guard along the edge of his desk while the trophy head of a deer had been mounted on the wall. All the place needed was a casting circle on the floor, and

Max thought the picture would be complete.

With three easy strides, he got behind the desk and rifled through the papers centered on the desk blotter. "Here," he said lifting an opened envelope. "Mr. Paulson Carroll. The guy has two last names." He sat in the chair and pulled out his phone. "See what you guys can find. Search everything."

"And what are you doing?" Irene said.

"I have his name now. I'm going to find where he lives."

A quick phone search online brought up seventeen instances of *Carroll*. That narrowed down to ten when he filtered only entries for *P Carroll*. But none of the listings had the full name of *Paulson Carroll* which meant Max would have to go through the remaining possibilities one by one until he found the man.

While continuing his work, Sandra and Irene attacked the office with the vigor of federal agents issuing a search warrant on a drug dealer. They toppled books, tossed drawers, and dumped trash cans with abandon.

Down to five possibilities, Max asked, "Any witchcraft?"

"Nothing," Sandra said. "But you've got to get the idea of witchcraft out of your head. This isn't going to be witchcraft. Not any that I know of."

Irene said, "That's right. Everything we've seen points to something different."

"The occult, then," Max said.

"If we're lucky. If not, then Mr. Carroll has gotten involved with something far darker. But all the speculation can wait until we have answers."

"You haven't worked with us for very long," Max said with a chuckle. "Speculation is our standard *modus operandi.*"

"In this case, you better wait till we get hard answers. Until we know what Mr. Carroll got himself involved with, if this is a spell gone bad or some form of devil's bargain or something even worse, well, we won't know how to handle it until then. Might as well stop spinning our wheels."

Tapping his phone, Max said, "Got him." Popping to his feet, he winked at Irene. "Let's go shed some light on Mr. Carroll. Get some of those hard answers."

Chapter 18

CRUISING UP OLD RURAL HILL ROAD, Max thought about how Drummond would handle the situation. They were in a residential area to the northwest of the city, straddling the border between poor and lower middle class — small homes with nice chunks of land because of the distance away from town. When they turned onto Ada Avenue and drove by Mr. Carroll's house — waist high chain-link fence surrounding the property — Sandra noticed a light on through the back corner window. Max had to drive a circuitous route in order to get to Don Avenue which paralleled Ada Avenue. He parked on the side and kept the engine idling.

"We need to approach this carefully," he said. "We've got surprise on our side. That's the best thing at the moment."

From the backseat, Irene said, "Until we know more, we have to assume Mr. Carroll could be dangerous. If he's the one who called the inhuman spirit, he might have other magic available to him. We should approach this like dealing with a dangerous, maybe even rabid animal."

"Yeah, but Sandra and I have met the man. I don't think he's a threat like that. He set us up with a trap that he didn't need to hang around for. Didn't want to be. He couldn't wait to get out of the house. I think we can trade-in on that."

"What do you have in mind?" Sandra asked.

"I want you and Irene to go knock on his door. We'll concoct a little tale — one he's expecting to hear, anyway. You tell him that things went bad at Reynolda House, that I got attacked by something you'd never seen before — something not a ghost. You tell him that I've been possessed."

"We act like we still think he's on our side and that were

trying to protect the secrecy of the job like he wanted."

"Exactly. While you two are doing that, I'm going to cut back through these yards and find a way inside Mr. Carroll's house. Hopefully, we'll get the drop on him."

She raised an eyebrow. *"Get the drop on him?"*

"What? Drummond's not here to say it. I figured somebody should."

Irene peered out the window. "You sure this'll work?"

"Drummond and I have done it several times. Of course, he has the ability to brain freeze a person and knock them out, but I'm a black belt. I think I can daze an old man long enough for us to grab him."

"It doesn't sound so easy, but if you're confident it'll work."

Sandra said, "It'll be fine."

She kissed Max's cheek as he opened the car door. When she eased into the driver's seat, he said, "Park right up at his house. Make him think you're not being cautious at all. But be cautious, please."

Once she drove away, Max turned to face the block of houses bordering Mr. Carroll's backyard. He crossed his fingers that Mr. Carroll would be the only insomniac up this night. He did not need for a sleepless neighbor to notice him prowling around. A concerned call to the police might mean the end of Drummond.

He stood still on the edge of the road and scanned the dark houses up and down the street. No lights on. No pale-blue flicker of a television. Nothing to indicate anybody did anything but sleep. He tried to think of another way to be sure until he realized he had been stalling.

Time to go.

Sticking to the grass to hide the sound of his feet, he scurried from shadow to shadow. Though late at night — or early in the morning depending on one's point of view — light pollution provided enough that he could see the large sticks and other obstacles. With great care to each step, he made his way between two houses and across the backyards.

Far faster than he expected, he came to Mr. Carroll's chain-link fence. He would have to hop over it, and that would make noise. Noise that Mr. Carroll would notice without doubt — Max could see the man's silhouette behind illuminated curtains of the back corner room.

He would have to wait. Wait and watch. His moment to act would come soon enough.

He heard music from behind. It grew louder — somebody revved the engine of a car as they rumbled through a late night joyride. The deep thump of bass and the grinding roar of a souped-up engine threatened to undo all of Max's careful nighttime sneaking. He had treated the backyards as behind enemy lines, yet this selfish driver plowed through the streets as if dancing through a summer field of flowers.

Max looked back in time to see the curtains pulling aside. He flattened to the ground. The cold earth pressed slick and cooled against his belly and cheek. He smelled the rich soil and dying leaves. Then the most welcome sound of the evening arrived — a doorbell.

The lights in Mr. Carroll's room turned off as he headed toward his front door to greet Sandra and Irene. Max gently rose to his feet and listened for their voices. This late at night, the sounds would carry — plus, Sandra had the sense to speak louder than normal.

Though he could not make out their words, he did hear those voices, and he needed nothing more. He moved fast. Pushing off the fence, Max vaulted over and rushed towards the side of Mr. Carroll's house. He tried the side door — locked. He tested the window next to it — locked.

Coming around back, he moved to the windows of the corner room. One had been left partially open. Either Mr. Carroll intended to close it before going to sleep or he left it open all night for the cool, autumn breeze. Didn't matter, though — Max would use it.

With a pocket knife, he cut along the bottom of the window screen as well as up through the middle. He then slid the window further up and crawled in.

"Why this is the most horrible change in circumstances,"

Mr. Carroll said from deeper in the house.

Max slithered onto the carpet. His knee bumped against Mr. Carroll's cane as he crawled toward the door. Peeking down the hall, he saw Mr. Carroll standing in front of Sandra and Irene exactly as they wanted — with his back to Max. Wasting no time, Max got to his feet and rushed forward. He brought up his arms, ready to clampdown tight around Mr. Carroll's neck, when the old man spun off into the kitchen with a laugh.

"I'm sorry, Mr. Porter," Mr. Carroll said as Max stumbled into Sandra. "I truly hate to see good people suffer needlessly. Of course, if you had simply done as expected, then I wouldn't need to do anything now. But here we are."

Standing in front of Sandra and Irene, Max gently pushed them back into the living room. Mr. Carroll stepped out of the kitchen, his kind face trembling with a twisted energy underneath.

"You all thought you would get me," Mr. Carroll said as he reached up to unbutton his shirt. "I watched you from the start. I saw you drive by my house, and I laughed as Max tried to secretly approach the house — ridiculous. You all thought you'd trap me. But I'm afraid you have it backwards. You are the ones that are trapped."

Max raised his fists. "I'm younger, and I'm stronger. There are three of us and one of you. This is not going to go how you want."

Mr. Carroll wagged a finger. "Don't be so sure."

Grabbing his shirt with both hands, he ripped the last buttons off revealing his hairless chest and protruding belly. Dried lines of blood ran down from numerous cuts. The man had carved his chest with a symbol of a spider cracked in two.

Max considered pulling out his gun, but he had yet to carry it loaded — never seemed enough time to properly train — and he doubted Mr. Carroll would fall for a bluff. He looked over his shoulder at Sandra. She shook her head. He glanced at Irene, she shrugged.

Great. Nobody had any idea what this symbol could do.

Mr. Carroll put out his hands like a demented grandpa

looking for a hug. He mumbled a phrase over and over. With a twisted smile, he arched his head back, and the wounds on his chest took on a purplish hue.

Max straightened. “Hell no.”

He thundered right up to Mr. Carroll and popped the man in the jaw. Mr. Carroll dropped back a few steps, and Max pressed forward. He pulled back for another punch. But Mr. Carroll’s eyes blazed fire — glowing red and orange fire.

Sweeping one hand to the side as if thrusting open a curtain, the old man snorted a laugh. Max felt an unseen force grab hold and drive him against the wall. His head cracked open the drywall covering him with white dust. Another swipe of Mr. Carroll’s hand and Max flew further down the hall, tumbling on the hard floor. The old man turned around slowly and strolled over his victim.

“My entire life people have underestimated me. I should not be surprised that you would be equally foolish. My parents were disappointed that I didn’t work hard enough in the fields — they had no appreciation for my intellect. When I got out from under them and went off to Harvard, my professors belittled me by assuming I was some backwoods hick. Those Northerners hear a fine, Southern accent and they all think we’re stupid. The rest of my life, everywhere I worked, they always thought less of me. And I could never quite get enough power in my positions to truly run things the way they should be run. Even at Reynolda House. I should have been brought in as the Head Curator. I know far more about that family and about Winston-Salem than all the rest combined. I studied it my whole life. But do they see that? No.”

Crawling backwards on the floor, Max looked up at this madman with his eyes burning bright and his chest glowing. “You’ve clearly got the power now.”

“Oh, yes. And once you are given up to the spirit, I will be stronger than all of them. Nobody will ever be able to put me—”

The light went out of his eyes. The glow on his chest disappeared. With his mouth locked open, he stared forward, his brow pulling down. And he collapsed.

Sandra stood behind him brandishing a table lamp.

Max grinned. "I love you."

"You better."

Irene peeked over Sandra's shoulder. "Nicely done. And as Drummond would say — quit loafing on the floor and we'll tie this fellow up before he wakes."

Chapter 19

THROUGHOUT THEIR YEARS SPENT TOGETHER, Max had enjoyed many moments in which he felt delight in knowing Sandra was his wife. Of course, there were the big accomplishments — the milestones reached, the challenges overcome, the fears faced. But he had long ago discovered that the little things often hit with a stronger sense of love, admiration, and yes, pride. Such a moment occurred when he dragged Mr. Carroll's heavy body towards a chair. Without a word, Sandra scoured the closets and a back room. A few seconds later, she returned and handed over a strong rope.

As Max tied up Mr. Carroll, Irene sauntered into the kitchen. He heard her opening and closing cabinets until she uttered a successful, "Yes." She came back carrying a bottle of Jack Daniels and a glass. As she sat on the couch, she noticed Max staring at her. "I'm sorry. Where are my manners? Did you want some as well?"

"It's all yours." He finished securing Mr. Carroll.

Standing with his hands on his hips, Max scanned the room. Not as cluttered as the Reynolda House office, but still a mess. Most of the furniture looked to be secondhand and the decorations on the walls could have been third hand. In fact, now that he looked closer, Max thought the place held more in common with a motel from the 1970s than a modern dwelling.

Knocking back the whiskey, Irene said, "Now that we've committed straight up breaking and entering as well as assault, what exactly are we planning to do?"

Max said, "We search this place. Top to bottom. Look for anything that might point us to how he called the inhuman spirit, what we can do about it, and most importantly, how we get Drummond back."

"First things first," Sandra said, wielding a carving knife.

Max put up his hands. "Whatever it is, I didn't do it."

"Not for you, hon. But don't tempt me." She crouched over Mr. Carroll and pressed the blade across his chest, marring the broken-spider symbol, thus destroying whatever power it might hold. Though Mr. Carroll whimpered, he did not wake.

"Okay, now that my wife is done mutilating a man, let's search the place."

The single-story house consisted of a living room, a kitchen, a bathroom off the hall, and two bedrooms — one which Mr. Carroll had used as an office. No basement. Only a crawlspace for an attic.

As Max searched the office, he wondered what went through Mr. Carroll's mind each day that he worked on the massive Reynolds estate. So massive that they gave away enough acreage to found Wake Forest University and still had tons of land leftover. The house itself — all those enormous rooms, multiple offices, spare bedrooms, playrooms, entire sections for parlor games, and even a bar and indoor pool — for a family of six. Most people would recognize the privilege that came with Reynolds success in tobacco. Most people accepted it on one level or another that some had more than others. Simple as that. But not Mr. Carroll. His ranting right before Sandra clocked him on the head had revealed a clue for Max to draw a sharp conclusion — the man's heightened sense of superiority must have cut deep. Every single day, Mr. Carroll had to be reminded of how little he achieved. And what had R.J. Reynolds done? Growing tobacco and marketing it. Mr. Carroll had gone to an Ivy League school. Mr. Carroll had pulled himself out of a poor upbringing. Mr. Carroll was smarter than everybody around him.

It must have driven him batty.

Enough so that the man embarked on a dangerous route, fiddling with forces well beyond his control. Some of that mindset proved evident in the books scattered about the office. Histories of witchcraft and treatises on old beliefs used by tribal medicine men. He had a book detailing herbs and herbal remedies as well as several anatomy books — most disturbingly, *The Merck Veterinarian Manual.* If the police ever had cause to search this place, they would have thought they had a budding serial killer on their hands.

Max opened the bottom drawer of the office desk. The book resting on top of a pile of papers screamed to him — this would be a special one. The first sign to shout out at Max was the cover. It lacked any markings, any title, anything to denote its purpose as if it wanted to hide or downplay that it meant something important. When he pulled the book out, he discovered it was less a book and more an album for photographs and newspaper clippings. Leafing through it, he discovered both of those items as well as numerous handwritten notes. Tucking the book under his arm, Max returned to the living room where Irene searched through a China cabinet and Sandra worked within earshot in the kitchen.

After explaining what he had discovered, he read some of the odd entries. "This is a clip from an article dated July 13, 1942. It's not clear what newspaper it came from. Mr. Carroll has a black-and-white photo of four people staring at the camera, all looking miserable. The article says —

> *Lula Belle Jones, a 36-year-old woman of Thomasville, lodged the charges against the four accused after she had previously preferred a formal charge of non-support of an unborn illegitimate child against Charles Stoneman, 19 years old.*

"Nineteen years to her thirty-six?" Irene said. "Sheesh, that's ... well, impressive for the woman. Wrong, of course, but still impressive."

Max stared at her for a moment, unsure of how to respond. He opted to continue reading the article.

> *The Jones woman testified that she had been living with a family at Thomasville and serving as nursemaid when*

> *she became expectant. Charles Stoneman was the father, she said. She quoted Charles as saying Mr. and Mrs. Wesley Stoneman would help her be rid of her embarrassment. She said Charlie and Mr. and Mrs. Wesley Stoneman took her to see Cornelia Moore, who prescribed that she take separate doses of quinine, camphor, and lemon extract. The Moore woman was paid five dollars. The next day, the doses were repeated — without any effect. She testified Charles then procured tablets for her and that Mrs. Stoneman advised another form of treatment, but all in vain. Then, Mrs. Stoneman contrived a crude surgical instrument from a coat hanger and advised her as to its use.*

Sandra said, "That's awful."

"Yeah," Max said, "But why would Mr. Carroll have cut out this particular article?"

Irene said, "Maybe he's related to Stoneman or this Moore lady."

"Here's another from 1961. Mr. Carroll wrote across the top — *Murder, David McCoy Leonard.* He pasted a notecard to the side of the article that says this was a preliminary hearing for Henry Lewallen, charged with first degree murder for killing his stepfather. The article reads:

> *Leonard, 44, was shot twice in the back, once in the chest, and once in the arm. Dr. M. E. Block said that either of the wounds in the back would have caused death. The slaying occurred at the Leonard home on a dirt road in the Johnsontown community. Sheriff Homer Lee Cox said the killing climaxed a family argument, and it was reported that wives of both men witnessed the shooting. Reports were that the argument concerned advances by Leonard to his stepson's wife. The Lewallens are parents of five children.*

And on this page there's no article but a grainy old picture of a train and several people in front of the engine. Mr. Carroll wrote that Anthony Hargrave nearly died when he was struck by a passenger train. Apparently, Hargrave was quite a drinker and right before the train arrived, he went up the railroad tracks and sat across the rails. Right in the way of the oncoming train."

"Suicide?"

"Maybe. The engineer saw him, sounded the whistle, and braked the train hard. Still hit Hargrave, though. Left a big hole in the guy, but he survived."

"Could be Hargrave had learned a little magic or had visited a witch and wanted to test out his new impervious nature. Or another relative of Mr. Carroll."

Flipping through the pages, Max said, "I don't get it. This entire album is filled with articles like this. Here's one from 1872, another from 1917, all way up into the 80s. Just skimming through the various reports and names, there's no way Mr. Carroll is related to everybody here. This is about something else."

Sandra stepped out of the kitchen. "The man's got a medicinal arsenal in here. I think he's been searching for a long time. Trying different avenues. A little herbalism, maybe some witchcraft, and eventually, whatever he actually used to call this inhuman spirit — clearly it worked."

Gesturing to the album, Max said, "You think this is part of that search?"

"Either that or he had a hobby of collecting strange and macabre tales of this city. Which is possible, but given how this night is going, I think we should look for common patterns."

Max sat on the threadbare couch and started at the beginning of the album. Picture after picture, article after article he searched for some common thread. 1903 — policeman Moyer Sink was attacked when escorting a prisoner named Shaver. The prisoner grabbed the policeman's billyclub and struck him over the head. As he made a run for it, Officer Sink shot Shaver twice — once in the ankle and once near the thigh. Both men survived and Shaver was recaptured lying in a ditch near the end of Center Street. 1914 — it was discovered that Davidson County continued to be one of the places in North Carolina that could not stop the tide of alcohol flowing through. A recent police raid discovered a wagon load of empty whiskey kegs proving how ineffective law enforcement had been. And then in 1967 — the Betty Crocker Homemaker of Tomorrow scholarship was announced in which senior high school girls were asked to write about all the phases of homemaking. Five thousand dollars was awarded in this national contest and the runner-up received four thousand.

"What the heck do any of these have to do with each other?" Max said to the album.

He had no idea how long he had been sitting there, but when Sandra came down the hall, he could not recall when she had left. She carried a large book and a larger smile.

"Here's a shocker," she said. "This is a primer for the occult from 1824."

"We heading back towards witchcraft?"

Sandra set the book on the stained coffee table. She opened the cover and pointed to the hand written words in the top corner — *The Brotherhood of the Rising, 1824.*

"Never heard of it. You?"

Sandra shook her head. "Irene?"

Looking over Max's shoulder, Irene said, "Let me see that album of news articles."

She came around and sat next to Max. As she flipped through the pictures, she glanced back at the book on the occult.

"What are we missing?" Max said.

With two fingers, she drummed at the words *The Brotherhood of the Rising.* "Look that up on your phone. Back then, there were a lot of these groups that sprouted up. Most were the equivalent of a college fraternity clothed in mystery and spooky semi-occult dressing. But some, of course, were the real thing. All of these groups would have their special traditions, ceremonies, secret handshakes, and symbols. A lot of them had symbols. See if you can find a symbol related to *The Brotherhood of the Rising*, please."

As Max tapped away on his phone, Irene continued looking through the album. She removed one photo — a black-and-white image of five men standing on courthouse steps in 1937. After a few more pages, she pulled out an article from 1902 that showed a grouping of women in front of a new schoolhouse. As she found several other photos and clippings to remove, Sandra started looking through this pile.

"Why these? I don't understand."

Max said, "I think I do. Look here."

He turned his phone toward Sandra. The Brotherhood of the Rising had a special symbol for its group — a symbol very similar to a spider broken in half. Sandra and Max gazed over at Mr. Carroll's carved chest.

Sandra said, "This group from the 1800s is still around?"

"Yes," Irene said. "Look at all these photos." Pointing at each one, Irene indicated small marks on hands and arms, and in one case, peeking over the high collar on a woman's neck. "With the poor quality of these photographs, I can't be sure that those marks are the same, although I do think that's why he was searching through all of this. Trying to narrow down the history of this group."

Max said, "What are we saying? Mr. Carroll is part of this Brotherhood of the Rising, and they called up this inhuman spirit?"

"Not quite. I don't think Mr. Carroll's a part of this group. Not yet. But I do think they were the ones to call the spirit."

"Why that is remarkably accurate," Mr. Carroll said, causing everyone to jump.

Chapter 20

THE SCENE MUST HAVE LOOKED RIDICULOUS. At least, Max thought so. Here he stood in another man's living room like a middle-management interrogator. His wife stood next to him, her arms crossed, gazing down with a disappointed look only a mother could wear. To Max's right — a tiny, bespeckled woman who could have easily been found in a fortune-telling tent at a carnival. And in front of them all sat an overweight, nearly retired museum curator with an occult symbol carved into his chest and a nasty gleam in his eyes.

"You're all going to die," Mr. Carroll said.

He had repeated variations on the sentiment several times already, and Max bored of it. "I think you've misjudged the situation. You've failed. When your colleagues at Reynolda House arrive for work in the morning, they'll learn what you did. You've lost your job. When you're friends at the Brotherhood of the Rising learn that you didn't succeed with the spirit, I don't think you'll be welcome there, either. In fact, your best chance at getting anything favorable out of this night is to help us."

Mr. Carroll snorted and spit in Max's direction. "You poor, blind fool. I shouldn't even be angry with you. So narrow-minded. So linearly focused."

"If I'm a fool, then educate me."

"You'll get your education when the spirit comes for your soul."

Sandra leaned close to Max. "Keep trying. I'm going to search his backroom once more. I found the Brotherhood book there, maybe I can find something else."

As she walked away, Irene stepped forward. "Mr. Carroll,

dear sir, I have to say that I am most impressed with what you have accomplished."

Max tried not to smile. Hopefully, Mr. Carroll's arrogance would blind him to this little bit of good cop/bad cop Irene had instigated.

"I'm serious," Irene said. "I've worked in many capacities as a psychic. I've seen ghosts and spirits, I've worked for police departments with missing children and for hotels with haunted rooms. All sorts of things. And yes, on rare occasion, I've even worked with the Porters here. But I've never come across a man capable of calling a spirit by himself. That is truly impressive."

"As it should be," Mr. Carroll said.

"What confounds me is the fact that you were able to do this without tapping into any form of witchcraft on the premises."

"I couldn't very well paint a casting circle on the Reception Hall floor, now could I?"

They both chuckled. Max noticed that Irene not only played along in the good cop role, but she elevated her Southern accent and word choice to match Mr. Carroll's old-time way of speaking. It had slipped in with such subtle grace that he doubted Mr. Carroll even noticed.

Max decided now would be a good time to bring out the bad cop once again. "Quit your laughing. I don't care how you got the spirit out there. What matters is that it's still out there and on the loose. You lost control of this thing, if you ever had it."

Mr. Carroll's face reddened as he strained against his bindings. "I did no such thing. That spirit could not leave Reynolda House until you folks messed things up by fighting back. You're the ones who ruined what was going to happen."

"What was that? Kill one of us?"

"Sadly, yes. But eggs and omelets. Eggs and omelets."

Irene tutted as she pushed Max to the side. "Never you mind him," she said, moving closer to Mr. Carroll. "He's been up all night and he's crankier than a mule on Monday. Besides, his wife is the real brains of the operation. She is quite an accomplished witch. I'm sure she'll figure out how to rein in your wayward spirit. That's why I'm more interested in how you created it. You know, back when I was young enough to have gentleman callers, there was one in particular who attempted what you have done. Thought he would impress me with such a feat. But the poor lad simply could not manage it. In fact, I can't think of any time I've ever seen somebody perform serious magic without the aid of witchcraft or at least the aid of a group working together."

Max made a show of pouting. "He's got a group. He's got the Brotherhood of the Rising."

"That's true. I suppose they are the ones really responsible for this."

Mr. Carroll's lip curled up. "Just because they aided in the creation of the spirit doesn't mean anything. I am the one entrusted with its control. I am the one who had to bring it all the way to Reynolda House. That spirit is nothing without me. And once it comes here, once it devours Mr. Porter or his wife, then you'll see. That's when you'll understand, and so will the Brotherhood."

Irene patted her cheeks. "I must say, all of this late-night chatter is making me thirsty. Would you care for a drink, Mr. Carroll?"

"No, ma'am. I can wait until I'm free."

"Max? You look thirsty. Why don't you join me in the kitchen?"

Max followed Irene but not before locking eyes with Mr. Carroll like two boxers right before the first round. Then Mr. Carroll's mouth opened into a wide grin. "Don't mind me," he said. "I ain't going to go anywhere."

The cramped kitchen had not changed decor since 1978. Orange cabinets and a Formica countertop met with yellowed linoleum on the floor. After only a few minutes in that room, Max thought he would need some of that era's heavy drugs in order to endure the assault on his senses.

"Did you catch all that?" Irene leaned against a lime green

refrigerator.

"Catch all what?"

"Mr. Carroll gave way more than he wanted to. You did a real good job throwing him off balance."

"Great. Thanks. But if he gave away how to take down this spirit, I missed it."

"For starters, he's not actually in the Brotherhood of the Rising. That's confirmed. Now, as I understand it, some of these occult groups — especially the more dangerous, more serious ones — they often have an initiation test."

"They summoned this thing as a test?"

"I think so. Mr. Carroll admitted that he did not summon the spirit himself. That he couldn't. I suspect that the current incarnation of the Brotherhood of the Rising called up an inhuman spirit and gave Mr. Carroll limited control of it. It's usually done through some sort of totem that acts as a leash on the spirit. If that's right, then he most likely was tasked to deliver a soul to the spirit. Do that and he's in the group. Plus, somebody gets their deal made. They might've told Mr. Carroll it would be him, but only those who actually did the summoning can make the deal. They probably neglected to tell him that part."

"This totem — what would it be?"

Irene wrinkled her nose. "Could be almost anything."

Max's mind had already drawn the connection. "Like a painting. One made to look as if it belonged in the gallery at Reynolda House."

Irene removed her glasses and made slow effort at cleaning them, keeping her eyes off Max. "You told me there was a bloody handprint behind the painting, and when you touched it, you had your experience that brought you to the Lake Porch. Is that right?"

"Yeah. When it was over, all the blood was gone. The painting's still there, though."

"That's cause the painting is no longer the totem. You broke that connection. Don't feel too bad — the spirit suckered you into it. It's actually Mr. Carroll's fault. When given a totem, the keeper of that totem must maintain control over it. Otherwise, it's like I'm untying the knot of string keeping a balloon around a child's wrist. The balloon flies away. The string's still attached but the balloon can go wherever it goes."

Max's legs grew heavy and his heart chilled. "Are you saying this inhuman spirit is attached to me now?"

"I wish. That would make everything easy. Understand that when Mr. Carroll left that painting on the wall in the gallery, he essentially tied that balloon loosely around a railing for anybody to come across. You're the one that untied the string."

"And the spirit is the balloon floating away."

"Now you see."

"Mr. Carroll put us in direct line to find it. He wanted us to find that painting. I doubt he knew the spirit would make the gallery bleed, but he wanted us to go in there — become victims of this thing."

"That's right. The spirit, knowing that nobody held its rope, lured you in further and tempted you to touch that handprint — to set it free. By the time I came to Reynolda House and we all went up into the attic, it had already gotten a taste of that freedom. There was no way it was going to respond to my simple requests. That's why it wants a body now. Before, it might've been satisfied with a soul, but no more. It wants everything."

"We already knew that."

"But now we know why."

Max rubbed his chin. "Does that help us?"

"I'm not sure," Irene said setting her glasses back on. "At least it gives us a line of inquiry when we start our interrogation again."

Max could not suppress a grin. "Were you ever a police officer?"

"Perhaps in another life."

He snickered as he thought over all that Irene had said. Her interpretation of events and how they pieced together worked well. His gut told him she was right. That would have to do. With four in the morning right around the corner, he did not have time for a deep dive research session to verify anything.

Except this wasn't witchcraft — the four o'clock witching hour did not matter. Unless it mattered for non-witchcraft reasons.

Leaning against the counter, Max said, "I have felt this urgency to stop the spirit and save Drummond this very night. Am I wrong? Can we slow down and take the time to do the research?"

Irene looked away. "The longer we wait, the more powerful the spirit will become. And the weaker Drummond will be. It's draining him."

"But even one day — Drummond's strong. I'm sure he could hold out one day."

"I know what you're doing. I know you want to fall back on your strengths. But the rest of you is fighting it. Whenever our instincts, our bodies, fight against our minds, then usually that means you're fighting against something the rest of you knows needs to be done."

Max pushed off the counter. "Are you saying my body somehow knows Drummond won't survive?"

"I don't know what your body is telling you. I know how to listen to mine. That's what a psychic does. And I can feel Drummond's strength waning." She took Max by the hands and gazed up at him. Her earnest eyes glistened with the tears she held back. "He will last till dawn. Maybe a bit longer, but not much."

"You know we'll do our best." Max tried to pull free, but Irene held tight.

"If we fail, we lose more than Drummond. With the dawn, that spirit will have all of his strength, and it will still be looking for a body and a soul. Because you connected to the totem, because you both fought it in the attic, it will come after you and Sandra, first. But if it can't have you or her, then it will gladly take someone else. This is the part people who summon spirits don't ever seem to understand — an inhuman spirit will consume a soul and its host body. Sometimes it'll take months, sometimes days. Then it will go find another. You understand?

If we don't stop this thing, it'll keep jumping from one person to the next. A lot of people will die."

Max checked the wall clock. "It's 3:45. Sunrise isn't until a little after seven. That gives us just over three hours. I guess that means we go back to interrogating Mr. Carroll."

Sandra thumped down the hall, went right by the kitchen, and fluttered back when she caught sight of her husband. She entered carrying the Brotherhood book as well as a yellow folder stuffed with various papers. She wore a bright smile.

Max clapped his hands together once. "You found something."

"You're darn right I did." She set the book and papers on the kitchen counter. "This folder is filled with Mr. Carroll's research on the Brotherhood. There are lists of former members, accounts of his attempts to contact some of these people, cross references to the information in the album you found, and more. Despite Mr. Carroll's faults, the man is meticulous at keeping notes. Thank goodness."

Max's heart sank. "This is an incredible find. If we had the time, I could spend a day or two searching through all of it, and I have no doubt I would uncover valuable information. But we've got to solve this tonight. If the sun rises and we haven't succeeded, Irene's made it clear to me that a lot of people will get hurt — maybe even killed. And we'll lose Drummond."

"Then it's a good thing you're married to me." She reached into the folder and pulled out a pamphlet with the broken spider symbol on the front. "This is a little welcome pamphlet that new members of the Brotherhood would get long ago. Don't know if they still do this — probably have a private site on the dark net now — but back in the day, this is how they did it."

Max opened up the pamphlet. Inside were the names and bios of key members of the Brotherhood. In the middle was an invitation to the next meeting on November 12, 1910. The bottom of the pamphlet had been burned.

Running his fingers along the charred edges, Max said, "So new members got this information, were expected to memorize what they needed, and burn the evidence."

"But not everybody followed through. Or in this case, it looks like somebody tried but was interrupted. Mr. Carroll's search for the Brotherhood led him to this. And this'll make you smile — he bought it on eBay."

"There's an address on the bottom."

She patted Max in the head. "You're so bright. I don't know what I'd do without you. Yes, there is an address, and I checked Mr. Carroll's notes for it. He's already looked into it. The building is an old warehouse that is still owned by descendants of Mr. Reginald Cotton. Look at that pamphlet again and you'll see Cotton is listed as the president of the Brotherhood in 1910."

Max's eyes widened. "You think they're still using it?"

"Only one way to find out."

Max felt a pleasant leap in his heart. A strange sensation of hope that had been missing the entire night. But then he thought of Mr. Carroll. That would be a problem.

As if reading his mind, and possibly she was, Irene said, "Don't worry. I'll stay back here and guard Mr. Carroll. I think there's still more information I can wean out of him. Maybe even find out about this warehouse before you get there."

"I'm not sure it's a good idea to leave you here. If he gets loose — well, you're a sweet little lady, but he's quite big."

Irene snickered as she opened up her purse. She pulled out a Smith & Wesson 29 revolver.

Sandra said, "You've got a gun?"

"I told you I'm a proper Southern gal through and through. My daddy taught me to shoot before I knew how to ride a bicycle. I'm better with a rifle, but in these close quarters, I suspect if he gives me any trouble, I won't have a problem putting holes in his kneecaps. Now, y'all get going. We've got a ghost to save and a spirit to stop."

As Sandra gathered together her research, Max smirked. "I'm beginning to understand what Drummond sees in you."

Chapter 21

BY THE TIME MAX AND SANDRA got in the car and headed back through the city, four o'clock had come and gone. With the sound of his tires gritting along the late-night road, Max noticed the puffiness around his eyes and the soreness in his muscles. Adrenaline could only propel him for so long.

"You know what's strange?" Sandra said.

"You're going to have to be a heck of a lot more specific."

"We went through another witching hour and nothing happened."

"Doesn't seem like a bad thing to me."

"I'm not saying it's bad, just strange. Every night, most people end up sleeping through numerous witching hours, and most nights it's nothing but another bit of time passing by. Makes me think about certain hauntings — the ones that occur at specific times. I mean do these ghosts sit around the house watching the clock, waiting for the exact same time to scare a person in the house?"

As Max turned onto East 5th Street, he said, "When you're dead and a ghost, you've got endless time. Waiting around for a specific moment might be the most exciting part of the day."

Sandra pressed her knuckles under her eyes in a fast motion that Max knew she hoped he had missed. But even if he had not seen that much, he could hear the emotion in her voice. "I never got the chance to ask Drummond about that."

"You will." Max had a catch in his throat and wondered if Sandra had noticed, too.

He slowed the car as they came near the end of the road where it merged with Salem Parkway. On the left side of the street, the Winston-Salem Journal had its main offices. On the right side, another road curved down amongst several warehouses and industrial buildings surrounded by woods. A flooring company, a place that sold baling equipment for farms, and several warehouses for distributors — from the outside of the building, Max could not figure out what they distributed. Probably best not to know. The address they sought led them further back, all the way to where the road turned to gravel and reached a dead end. To the left stood an old brick building with no signage. The windows had been boarded over, and the wide double-doors at the front had a locked chain to prevent entry.

In the lot overgrown with weeds, two practical sedans had been parked. Max shut off his headlights and peered at the darkened building — no sign of light peeking through the cracks. He flicked the headlights back on, performed a three-point turn, and drove down two warehouses.

Parking in an empty, freshly paved lot, Max took a deep breath. "Make sure we have everything we'll need."

Sandra patted her bag. "How quickly you forget — I'm a mama now. I always have everything we need."

Strolling toward the Brotherhood warehouse, Sandra locked her arm around Max's. The cold night air and her sweet smell reminded him of moments from their youth walking to her door after a date.

"It's strange the thoughts nights like this bring," he said.

"Or don't bring. I've been so consumed thinking about Drummond that I haven't thought about the boys in hours. You haven't mentioned them, either."

Max stopped in the middle of the road. "You're right."

"See that? We care so much about Drummond being in danger that it's taken over our thoughts. We know the Sandwich Boys are safe where they are, so we don't have to freak out about them for now."

Resuming his walk, Max said, "It's the *for now* part that's worrisome."

"You're still obsessing about this?"

"Not about my mother and our family. I'll have plenty of time to obsess about that another day. But the entire drive here,

I've been thinking about what Irene said. If we fail tonight, this will not only destroy Drummond, but the inhuman spirit will come after us. We already know that it can't defeat us when we're together."

"But then it will go after somebody else — you think it'll go after the boys."

"Why wouldn't it? The boys are connected to us. I don't claim to understand how an inhuman spirit thinks, but it certainly seems to behave with some sense of connection to its victims. I wouldn't be surprised if it went after the boys as an act of revenge against us."

"Things won't come to that. We're going to stop the spirit and save Drummond. Simple as that."

They picked up their pace and entered the warehouse parking lot. Max rested his hand on the hood of each car — cold. That much was good.

He suggested they walk around the building to get a sense of the place. Though there were a couple of amber streetlights, the Brotherhood warehouse stood far enough back that shadows shrouded most of it.

Max and Sandra flicked on their flashlights but kept the beams low to the ground — enough to see where they stepped but, hopefully, not to attract attention.

The ground sloped downwards, nothing too steep, and exposed the stone foundation of the building. Max paid particular attention to any window or door they walked by. No strange lights came out. No sense of movement inside. The place looked dead.

When they finished their tour, they checked the locked chain around the front entrance. "How are your lock-picking skills?" Max asked.

"No better than when you asked me earlier this evening. I'm definitely no Irene Beck. You probably have more experience doing this than me."

"Okay, keep a lookout. I'll see what I can do."

Holding the penlight in his mouth, Max turned the padlock over to inspect the keyhole. Not that he knew what to look for but he wanted to get an idea of how hard it could be. Turned out — very hard.

"I can't do this one."

"Around back, I spotted a window that wasn't boarded up — probably because it was pretty high off the ground. If we break that open and you hoist me up, I might be able to get inside."

The plan did not sit well. Not because Max thought Sandra would fail, but because it meant that she would have to roam around the warehouse looking for an entrance to open while being alone the entire time. Splitting up with Drummond never bothered Max too much — after all, if Max ran into trouble, Drummond could pass right through a wall for a rescue. But if Sandra came upon any problems while inside, Max would be helpless to do anything useful.

"No risk, no reward," she said as she headed towards the back corner.

Max hustled to catch up. "Hold on. Let's think this through."

"Nothing to think through, hon. Drummond needs us. The boys' lives could be in danger. This is our way inside."

She stooped over to pick up a rock. About ten feet above, Max found the corner of the large window. As he shined his penlight on the area, Sandra hefted the rock into the air.

First try — bullseye.

The glass shattered making a loud noise that echoed into the forest. Both Max and Sandra held still as the sound carried away. They waited. A full minute went by before either was willing to move.

Then Sandra jumped into action. Less than five minutes. That's all the time she needed. After giving her a boost up to the ledge, she shimmied through the window, and before Max had time to really let his imagination wander into picturing her death, she whispered his name. Around the back corner, her hand waved him on. Max followed and discovered that she had opened a narrow door leading into a wood-paneled hallway with several small offices on either side.

The triumph on her face brightened the area almost as much as her flashlight. "You're incredible," Max said.

With a quick and seductive lick of her lips, she said, "Play your cards right and you may find out how incredible."

Max gently pushed her shoulder toward the hall. "Let's save Drummond first."

Before letting go, his hand lingered on her back to say *thank you.* Though merely a few words of levity and a wink at the promise of a hot evening to come in a few days, his wife had managed to sweep aside some of the pressure that had been gripping him the entire night.

"Look at this," she said entering the office to the right.

Max followed and had to admit that no matter what he thought he might find, he would never have guessed this. Two large folding tables had been set up in an L-shape. Three computers formed a giant workstation complete with four widescreen monitors. Three of the monitors had been set to splitscreens of several video feeds from cameras — presumably stationed throughout the building. The fourth monitor on the end had an audio program up and running. Numerous wires snaked out the back of these electronics in a jumbled mess that led through the far wall. On the left end of the monitors, a small metal box clicked a steady rhythm. It had a row of lights running green to red as well as a needle gauge. Whatever it monitored appeared to be barely registering. A larger, boxy piece of equipment filled up the remaining space on the table — blinking red and green lights as well as dials with digital numbers giving constant readouts.

Max checked through the various camera feeds — hallways, the office next door, the front lobby, as well as several camera feeds labeled *Main Floor.* However, the main floor feeds were all dark.

"This doesn't really feel like security surveillance, does it?" Max asked.

"No. This is something else."

"We can see about everywhere in the building, I think. But why would you want to? The place is empty."

"Except we can't see in the main room. How much you want to bet that's where we need to go?"

"Yeah. Because unless one of these rooms is saturated in blood, the room that's all blacked out has got to be the one for us."

Sandra gave Max a quick smack in the rear. "You gotta love this job. Let's go."

The hallway ended in a narrow staircase that led up to the main floor. As they climbed the stairs, the pale beam from the flashlight casting a ghostly pall, Max noted how clean everything looked. For a building supposedly abandoned for several years, not only did they have the electricity to power an entire surveillance room, but somebody kept the stairs swept clean and the cobwebs from forming in the corners.

Like the stairwell and the offices, the main floor had also been well kept. Though cavernous and empty, Max found the place all too familiar. Throughout his years with the Porter Agency, he had spent enough time in warehouses late at night to get a feel for them. They had their own special vibe — a hollow sensation similar to the empty streets during the late-night hours or an airport terminal after the last flight had gone. People who worked at an amusement park or any crowded venue knew the feeling — everything sounded off-kilter without the expected bustle. Warehouses were no different. And completely empty warehouses — not even an old crate or disused piece of equipment — doubly so.

In fact, only two offices broke up the monotony of the emptiness — one on either end of the main floor. Both offices had a typical plate glass window so that the managers could observe the warehouse while doing their work.

As they meandered into the center, the echoes of their footsteps gave the room an even larger feel. Max smelled the remnants of something that had been burnt. Running his light across the open space, the answer became clear and disturbing.

"Is that what I think it is?" he asked.

Sandra squatted and brushed her hand over the spot Max highlighted. "Candle wax," she said.

They backed up and spread their lights as wide on the floor as they could manage. Before Max even registered what he looked at, Sandra's reaction prickled his skin.

"Oh, crap," she said.

A large red triangle had been painted on the floor. Three circles also had been painted — one around each point of the triangle. A fourth circle of chalk took up the center of the triangle, and The Brotherhood of the Rising's broken spider symbol rested neatly within that circle.

Max said, "I know you and Irene keep insisting that there is no witchcraft with this inhuman spirit, so forgive me for sounding stupid — isn't this witchcraft?"

"It certainly wants to look like witchcraft. But everything I've learned about the art suggests this would not actually accomplish anything. Circles and triangles — you know those well. But just throwing down shapes doesn't make spells happen. This configuration is pointless without more to it. And I know we found evidence of candles, but I don't see anything else associated with casting a spell. No words in any language, no salt, nothing of purity, nothing to focus the concentration. Even blood magic would have bowls to collect the blood." She caught Max's raised eyebrow. "Don't worry, honey. I read about blood magic — doesn't mean I'm going to start practicing it."

"Well, if the Brotherhood is responsible for calling up the spirit, and if you're right that this is not witchcraft, then what is it?"

"Ceremonial, perhaps. Or maybe older magic."

"Older?"

"Witchcraft isn't the only study out there that's been able to tap into supernatural forces. Lots of old religions had blood sacrifices — what do you think those were for?"

"Are you saying that all religions are actually some older form of attempts at magic? That they evolved into witchcraft?"

Sandra chuckled. "Sometimes your intuition leaps a bit too far. I'm not saying any of that. I am saying, some religions — not all — have indeed grown out of magical practices. The

Aztecs, for example."

"The Aztecs were a precursor to witchcraft?"

"We don't really have time for me to give you a full lecture on the subject, but sacrificial blood ceremonies were used to enhance power, strength, longevity, good harvest, healthy procreation, and a whole host of other things. Some of those practices which were incorporated into religious doctrine were real. Magic didn't come out of nowhere, and while many of the spells died out or were relegated to becoming myths, some of the spells remained. Those who continued to practice the old traditions became outcasts, and eventually, many of the practices led towards witchcraft. Really, witchcraft is nothing more than the formalized evolution of all these ancient practices. The point is that these markings on the floor, like the Brotherhood itself, date back hundreds, maybe thousands of years. It's possible that these are authentic."

"If it is, then it's not witchcraft but some other form of magic."

"That's right. And other forms of magic have their own rules. Rules that I probably don't know."

The sound of heavy wheels crunching gravel reached Max's ears. He shut off his flashlight and motioned for Sandra to do the same. They held still.

Car doors slammed shut. Footsteps and muffled talking. In the dark, Max strained to hear over his own heartbeat.

When he caught the sounds of the padlock being worked open and the chains removed, he grabbed Sandra's hand. They bolted.

"Back office," he said. Racing right by the stairwell to the far end, Max crossed his fingers that the manager's office door had not been locked. As they came upon it, he dared to turn on his flashlight — the door stood slightly ajar. Now he had to hope the hinges didn't whine.

They stepped in — quietly, thank goodness — and closed the door behind them. No furniture in the office. Nothing to hide behind but the wall. They crouched under the plate glass window, and Max shut off his flashlight once more.

Before he had a chance to fully settle, the hanging lamps running rows down the warehouse floor lit up with a loud clank. Peeking from the bottom corner of the office window, Max saw the floor had two large cameras on tripods situated opposite each other and focused on the triangle symbol. A third camera had been mounted on a scaffold near the side wall.

Footsteps. A lot of them. Keeping low, Max watched as a large group of people entered — he counted seven.

At the head, a stark woman with stringy blonde hair marched toward a folding table set up off to the side. Max had missed that in the dark, but it stood out with the lights on. When she reached the table, the woman set down a leather satchel and a small handgun.

The next six people following in clearly belonged to two separate, vastly different groups. One woman with buzzed, punk white hair that stood out against her dark skin and two bulky men — one chubby with a goatee, one muscular with a heavy five o'clock shadow — belonged with the blonde woman. These four were in charge. Max assumed they were members of the Brotherhood. The other three — two women and one man — had their arms tied behind their backs and their eyes darting around like mice desperate for an escape.

Sandra scrunched up at the other corner to peek out. She gasped. "That's Libby."

The moment Sandra spoke the name, Max recognized one of the hostages — Liberty "Libby" Broward. A paranormal researcher, a ghost hunter, a stern Japanese woman who had worked with them on a case involving a haunted brothel five or so years back.

"What's she doing here?" Max whispered. "After everything that happened, she said she was out of the business. Never wanted to be part of it again."

"Guess things changed."

While Goatee kept the hostages standing together at gunpoint, the rest of the Brotherhood joined the blonde lady at the table. From the satchel, they pulled out three bowls —

ornate and old looking things. Relics, really. The kind of highly-valued ceremonial bowl used in blood magic. To further confirm Max's dark suspicions, next to each bowl, Punk Girl set a long, sharp knife.

Max shook his head. "This is bad."

Chapter 22

MAX REMEMBERED LIBBY BROWARD as an organized and controlling young woman. A touch of OCD, probably, but she carried herself with confidence and a brutal sense of caution. Dealing with all the people claiming to be psychics, haunted, or some variation of the theme had turned Libby into a person who found trust difficult. Max understood. He had to battle those thoughts as well.

But being at the mercy of the Brotherhood had already broken her. She wore a sunken, lost expression. Little noises jolted her senses like an abused puppy. Yet whenever she glanced back at her team, Max saw that confidence return. She wanted them to still follow her. She wanted them to feel safe.

"Ms. Sinauer, there has been a big misunderstanding," Libby said with a bit of calm. Max found that encouraging, though the two members of her team inched away from her. "There's no need for all these threats. We're not here to harm you. You asked for us, and we came to help."

One of Libby's team, a bony man who must have lived on caffeine and pizza, stifled a cry as he wiped his damp face. The woman next to him held her composure far better, but even from behind the glass in the office, Max could see the quiver of her chin.

With a practiced move, Ms. Sinauer tied her hair back into a tight ponytail. She turned to face everybody. In a voice far smoother than her features, she said, "You were brought in to witness an exclusive event. We wanted it documented for the first time ever. We made it clear that you were never to make a copy of these events nor would you ever be able to speak about this night. You even signed an NDA — one that stated plainly the penalty for breaking our trust would be severe."

"We've honored that contract. We didn't make any copies. We haven't spoken to anyone about this. We haven't done anything to break your trust."

As Ms. Sinauer continued to speak, she stood straight with her arms loose at her sides. She only moved her head enough to keep constant watch on everybody. "Did you know that women were only allowed into the Brotherhood of the Rising starting in 1967? My grandmother, Paula Peterson, was among the first. My mother, Jennifer Wolfe, followed in her footsteps. And I have continued the tradition. I was in the Brotherhood before I got married. In fact, I met my husband through the Brotherhood."

Libby looked at the two men. "I didn't realize —"

"One of them? Never. When you work for an organization like the Brotherhood, you have to accept certain responsibilities. In that respect, it's a bit like the Army. You get stationed places, and you are expected to go, no matter what. For the moment, I'm here and my husband is not. He has his own assignments."

"I'm sorry to hear that."

Max cringed. Libby needed to stop talking. Every time she interrupted, Ms. Sinauer bit back and her fingers curled into claws. Max didn't think that kind of restraint would last long.

"I know you're frightened," Ms. Sinauer continued. "You did something wrong and you don't want to face the consequences. It's a common problem with us Americans. Many of us have benefited from being top dog for so long that we've forgotten what it's like to struggle. We have forgotten what it's like to sacrifice our pleasures, our wants, and our needs in order to survive. I think that's part of why the Brotherhood split my husband and I for a little while. It's a sacrifice necessary to make us appreciate each other. That's what I'm trying to explain to you. You are in the presence of something greater than you, more important as a whole than as an individual. I realize that's not very American, not very patriotic. We do value our independence. But in order to accomplish great things, we have to work as a whole unit. No individual made it to the moon. That was a group effort. That is what the Brotherhood is about."

Ms. Sinauer finally moved. She turned back to the table, picked up one bowl and a knife, and walked in a direct line to the first circle at the corner of the triangle. She set the bowl and knife in the middle of the circle, stepped back, and gazed at them as if she had created a great work of art. She then gestured toward the circle and strolled back to the table. As she moved, Goatee escorted Libby's barely composed teammate to that circle.

"I made it clear to you all," Ms. Sinauer continued, "that when you agreed to witness this night, you also agreed to become part of the Brotherhood."

Libby stiffened, her jaw jutting out even as her legs shuddered. "That is not true. We never agreed to join your group — only to join this evening, to record your ceremony."

Ms. Sinauer giggled as she picked up the second bowl and knife. She tinged the bowl with the knife as she walked over to the next circle. "Do you really expect me to believe that you are that naïve?"

"I expect you to honor our contract. We were asked to do a simple job, and that's what we've been trying to do. It's not our fault you couldn't control your man." Libby's eyes flared at the severity of what she had said, but she impressed Max by not apologizing.

"Yes, Mr. Carroll — your accomplice in all this." Ms. Sinauer waved her hand again, and Shadow pushed the man on Libby's team to the second circle.

"We never met Mr. Carroll until tonight. You are the ones who —"

"Enough." With a sharp motion of her head, she had Punk Girl move Libby to the last circle. She then walked over to the table for the final bowl and knife. "Like you, Mr. Carroll had a specific agenda for being here. And while you may have been confused about your purpose, he was not."

"Then why are you punishing us? We didn't betray you.

Frankly, he didn't either. He wanted to impress you."

"What he does and does not want means nothing. Somebody must be held responsible, and I've chosen you."

Sandra sat back on the floor. Whispering, she said, "These people are crazy."

"You're surprised?" Max said. "I don't think anybody sane joins a group called The Brotherhood of the Rising. Not when they promise to call up inhuman spirits."

Max could see on Sandra's face that she did not listen. Even her comment was not consciously uttered. Her narrowed eyes and firm jaw told him everything — she was thinking, calculating, working out her next move.

Libby dropped to her knees and brought her hands together. Her cheeks glistened with tears. "Please, don't do this. Gene and Angie have nothing to do with any of it. You blame me? Fine. At least, let them go."

Ms. Sinauer shook her head. "They work for you. That's all the guilt they need to have. Besides, we want their blood."

She snapped her fingers. Shadow snatched up the knife and slit open Gene's neck. He then dropped the blade and brought the bowl up to collect Gene's draining life. Libby and Angie screamed.

Max turned to Sandra. "We can't let them do this."

"No kidding. You think I've been sitting here singing songs in my head?"

"No, I think you have a plan, and I'm saying now would be a good time to tell me."

Sandra crawled forward and opened her bag. She pulled out a small container of salt and a piece of black chalk. "You know what I need."

Max scurried toward the office door. "I'll buy as much time as I can. Please, hurry." He slipped out the door and watched as Ms. Sinauer waited for Libby and Angie to stop blubbering. With everyone's attention on the crying women and Gene's blood pouring into a bowl, Max figured he would never get a better distraction. Staying low, he dashed across the small gap to the stairwell. As softly as possible, he placed each foot down on the stair treads, hoping to avoid a single creak. Though the women bawling behind him covered most of his noise, he had no idea when they might stop.

When he reached the bottom, he dashed down the hall and into the surveillance room. Not surveillance — ghost hunting. Paranormal research. This was Libby's set up.

Sitting down at the bank of computers, he cracked his knuckles and started waking up the equipment. "Okay, let's see what kind of chaos I can make."

Chapter 23

WASTING NO TIME, Max started clicking the mouse and tapping the keyboard. From the monitors, he could see Libby, Angie, and the Brotherhood. One of the screens flashed off of the surveillance cameras and brought up the various programs running. He started clicking through them and found the camera operations.

With little trouble, he gained control of the two tripod-mounted cameras. He started spinning them around. Right when he decided that wasn't going to be enough, Shadow said, "What's going on with those?"

The man's voice registered in a waveform on the audio screen. The scaffold camera displayed a wide view of everybody standing at the triangle symbol. Max watched as Ms. Sinauer walked over to one of the spinning cameras.

To Libby, she said, "Why is it doing this?"

"I don't know. I'm not the camera expert. You just killed him."

This wouldn't be enough. The Brotherhood would eventually shrug off the cameras as malfunctioning. They had more important things to do. Max needed something bigger.

He next found controls for lighting equipment — most of it attached to the cameras. While he knew paranormal investigators focused mostly on infrared and other nonvisual color spectrums, as long as a fill light had been attached to the cameras at some point, Max had a chance. He toggled on every lighting function he found on the screen.

"Now what?" Goatee said.

From the stationary camera, Max observed the two spinning cameras flickering little lights. Not a big fill light, but merely red and green pinlights to acknowledge different modes coming on and off. Still, it got Goatee's attention. Bonus — each shift in lighting mode came with a beeping noise.

Searching for another way to confuse the Brotherhood, Max clicked on the button marked *Sound.* He had hoped it would allow him to make spooky noises through the microphone, but instead, Metallica's "Creeping Death" blasted out of all the computer speakers at once.

He jolted, sending the mouse clattering to the floor. The battery popped out and rolled off to the side. Max tried to shut the music down from the keyboard, but he couldn't find the right combination. He scrambled across the floor, swiping up the battery and the mouse and jumped back to the table. Two attempts and he fumbled the battery into the mouse. Smashing the whole thing back onto the table, he swept the mouse around the screen until a few panicked clicks later, he managed to shut off the music.

But he heard the steady clop of somebody coming down the stairs.

In the seconds it took Shadow to arrive, Max considered making a break for it — burst into the hallway and blitz down toward the exit. Shadow would give chase, and if Max managed to get outside, he could swing around to the front, kick open the main door, and disrupt things on the floor. Cause enough trouble, and he might be able to —

But Shadow might simply startle at Max's sudden appearance in the hall and open fire. An outcome Max wanted to avoid.

Without any other doors or windows to the surveillance room, Max saw no better alternative than to raise his hands and wait. Good thing, too. Shadow cornered around the door brandishing a hefty silver handgun — the kind of thing that would make Clint Eastwood jealous.

He took a quick look over at Max and holstered his weapon. Max tried not to be offended.

"Come on," Shadow said. "Don't make this hard on yourself."

Max walked over. "May I put my hands down? I promise not to do anything stupid."

Shadow nodded, and as Max lowered his hands, he discovered that Shadow liked cologne — a lot of it. Walking by the man in order to head up the stairs, Max coughed as the air took on an acidic taste and a slick scent not recognizable as anything natural.

He climbed the stairs with lethargic steps until Shadow pushed him in the back. Every second mattered. Not only to give Sandra all the time she required, but Max needed to figure out something to say, some way to stall Ms. Sinauer longer.

Why am I always one who has to stall in these dangerous situations? A thought for another time.

"You know," he said over his shoulder, "your Brotherhood has quite a history."

"Say one more word and I'll break your neck. Now get in there."

Not the response he had hoped for.

As he walked onto the main floor, Max fought every urge to glance at the office window. Sandra was there. He knew it. He trusted her. Looking in that direction would not change a thing.

Ms. Sinauer's small eyes zeroed on Max. "Who are you?"

"You?" Libby said.

Ms. Sinauer looked to Libby. "You know him?"

"I'm Max Porter. I'd offer to shake hands, but I think this big guy behind me would shoot me through the back of the head."

Shadow snickered. "I found him in that room these people set up. He was playing with the computers."

Ms. Sinauer continued to knock her attention between Max and Libby. In the end, she decided Libby would be the better route to go. "Who is he?" she asked.

"Nobody," Libby said.

"Hey," Max said, a bit of genuine hurt rushing through him.

With a sharp finger pointed in his direction, Ms. Sinauer said, "You do not speak." She turned to Angie. "Who is he?"

As if each word caused mental anguish, Angie said, "I don't

know. I've never seen him. Honest. Please, please, please, don't—"

Ms. Sinauer went back to Libby. "I'm only going to ask once more."

Libby's face wrinkled. Clasping the top of her head as she tried to make sense of Max's sudden appearance, she said, "He's nobody. He doesn't work with me. He's just another paranormal investigator. I met him years ago on a case. I haven't seen him since. I don't know why he's here."

Ms. Sinauer bounced her fist on her jaw. She did not speak for a moment, and nobody dared to interrupt her thoughts. When she finally broke the silence, her voice had taken on a far more sinister tone. "This night was supposed to be special. This night was going to be a triumph. Most importantly, this night was to be a secret. Nobody knew this was going to happen except those of us in this room and Mr. Carroll. Yet you want me to believe that this man, a man you know but apparently have not seen in years, just happened to come upon us." She shook her head as if it pained her to consider her next words. "You're not taking me seriously."

A nod and Goatee picked up his knife. Angie cried out and spun in an attempt to escape, but Goatee held her firm.

"Don't do this," Libby said, struggling against Punk Girl's firm grip.

But it was done. Before she had even finished speaking, Goatee had run his blade across Angie's neck to fill the bowl with her blood.

Covering her mouth, Libby dropped to her knees. Punk Girl let her fall, salivating at her pain. Libby's body heaved even as no sound escaped her. Ms. Sinauer crouched in front of her. "Perhaps you are willing to talk now."

Max swallowed against the gorge in his throat. He had an idea of what to say, but if his voice betrayed any of the disgust he felt, Ms. Sinauer would ignore him. He closed his eyes and pictured Drummond, PB and J, and Sandra. He could do this.

Forcing a chuckle that sounded thin in his ears, he said, "Wow, I suspected the Brotherhood was weak, but I didn't realize you were this pathetic."

Ms. Sinauer jumped to her feet. "How dare you."

"What else would you call this? You've been planning on killing everybody all along. You have to in order to get the blood you need for whatever this ceremony is going to do, yet you feel it necessary to play mind games with this young woman. You're taking pleasure in mentally torturing her. That's weak."

"Perhaps my men can show you how weak we are."

Max put up one hand like an old professor acknowledging an even older argument. "I have no doubt your people could break all my bones, make me bleed, heck, even kill me. But that is my point. See, you are clearly new around here. That's why you don't know my name. But you start asking around and you'll find the Porter Agency is well-known in certain circles. The kinds of circles you're playing in right now. I've faced some serious witches in my time, and I'm sorry but the Brotherhood doesn't measure up."

With rage building in her face, she said, "You really think insulting us is your best play?"

Max noticed a slight shaking in his fingers, so he quickly stuck his hand in his pocket. "It's not that I'm trying to be rude. I'm trying to be practical — for you. The Brotherhood of the Rising has a long history. That's obvious even from the little bit I've learned about you. But all organizations rise and fall over the years. I've seen covens that were around for centuries torn apart in one night. From the way this night has gone for you, it seems fairly clear that the people in this room are the limit of the Brotherhood membership. I'm not even sure I believe you have a husband off on some other Brotherhood mission. And the fact that you're not protesting that idea suggests I'm right. No, don't bother now. Even if you can prove he exists, there's clearly no more to the Brotherhood than what's right here. Oh, except for Mr. Carroll."

"He is not one of the Brotherhood."

"He certainly wants to be."

"Oh, I see now. You were his intended victim. You be

careful, Mr. Porter. Keep insulting me and I'll see that our spirit comes back here and possesses you."

"Already tried it once. Didn't take. Funny thing about summoning and all of that — each spell, each practice, they all have their own specific rules. Some of the fine print is ridiculously difficult to find, but you have to know it, or else you end up with a mess like the one you guys are in right now. I mean, that is why you're trying to get all this blood, right? You're not actually planning on calling another spirit. You want to get this one back on its leash. Send it back to where it came from before it comes after you all."

Max had no idea if that was their plan, but it sounded accurate. It also made him seem more knowledgeable about summoning spirits. From Ms. Sinauer's hesitation, he figured the lack of experience caused her to doubt. All the better.

But then she bent down in front of Libby and lifted the ceremonial knife. Max's pulse picked up. Caressing the carved handle, she raised her eyebrows. "You talk a lot yet say very little. I don't think there's anything of value I can get from this conversation. In fact, the only thing you mentioned is that you are somebody important in the paranormal world. Yet you don't seem that important. Libby barely knows you, and Angie didn't know you at all. You're all alone. Tell me again — how is it that you are so important?"

"For one thing, I fought off your inhuman spirit from possessing me. That ought to give you pause."

She mocked a thoughtful wrinkle in her brow. "Nope." She snapped her fingers at Punk Girl who forced Libby back to her feet. "If you want to say goodbye to each other, now would be the time."

Ms. Sinauer raised the knife to Libby's throat and paused. Her mouth opened wide and her head turned up for a moment. Everyone stared at Ms. Sinauer, wondering what she intended to do when the woman thrust forward with a loud sneeze. The force jostled her body hard enough that she dropped the knife.

With an embarrassed laugh, she said, "The dust in this place must be getting to me. I'm so sorry." She bent over, retrieved the knife, but never had time to stand straight. Another heavy sneeze erupted from her body, the sound bouncing about the large room.

"Are you okay?" Punk Girl asked. "You want me to get you—"

Punk Girl sneezed — a high-pitched squeak.

From behind, Max could hear Shadow sniffle. The sniffling grew louder until finally a huge roar sent Shadow stumbling back several steps.

Goatee saw all three of his brethren unable to stop sneezing. "What's going on?"

Folding his arms, Max said, "I think you call it magic."

Goatee pulled back a fist and stormed towards Max. But the sneezing affliction struck him, too.

"Sandra, come on out," Max said. "You got them all."

Sandra rushed out of the office and embraced Max. As they hurried across to Libby, Ms. Sinauer reached out toward them, but another sneeze brought her to the floor.

While Max untied Libby, Shadow straightened and took three threatening steps. But his eyes watered from all the sneezing and he accidentally stepped on Angie's blood bowl. The bowl cracked like an egg, and slick blood washed across the floor. Shadow slipped and fell hard, his head smacking with a loud conk.

"Let's go, let's go," Sandra said.

As she dragged Libby by the hand, Max grabbed one of the ceremonial knives. He hurried to follow his wife out of the building.

In the parking lot, he found three cars. The two he had seen before, but the newest one — a red minivan — still felt warm. Like a warrior facing a defeated foe, Max strode up to the red car and brandished the ceremonial knife. He proceeded to stab the knife into each of the four tires.

"Are you okay?" Sandra said to Libby.

As Max crossed the lot to the next car and stabbed more tires, he caught the horrified look in Libby's eyes.

"No, I'm not okay," she said. "What kind of stupid question

is that?"

Before her stress could mount into an erupting volcano of tears, Max tried to shift their attention. "Why sneezing?" he asked. "And why did you take so long? I mean I stalled, but you were cutting it close."

Wrong tactic.

Sandra put her hand on her hip as she glared. With a measured voice — never a good sign from Sandra — she said, "You keep acting like I've been studying witchcraft my entire life. I'm still getting to know what I can do. And for your information, I was trying to put them to sleep, not start an orgy of sneezing. I'll have you know that to make a spell affect those four and not you or Libby isn't easy. At least, not for me. Especially when I don't have access to my full array of witchcraft materials. Not to mention, I haven't slept. I'm exhausted. You should be thanking me."

Max slashed the tires on the last car. As the air hissed out, he walked up to Sandra and hugged her tightly. "You're right. I'm sorry. Thank you."

"It's okay. I think we're all a little stressed."

Stepping back, he asked, "How long will they be sneezing?"

"No idea. But I don't think we should stick around."

To Libby, Max said, "We parked down a few lots. Where's your car?"

She pointed directly behind Max as the hiss of tires died out.

With a sheepish grimace, he said, "Oh. Sorry. Better you come with us anyway. We all need to talk."

"I'm not going with you," Libby said, less forceful, more incredulous. Her arms tightened around herself.

"This isn't over. Those crazy people in there started something terrible, and we've got to stop it. Plus, one of our friends is in danger because of all this. So you are coming with us right now. We're going to go sit down someplace and find out what you know. It might save a lot of lives."

"I said I'm not doing it. I shouldn't have been here in the first place. I want none of this." Libby's voice rose in pitch. "You can't make me. Everybody's trying to make me do one thing, then another, and now Angie is dead, Gene is dead, there's blood and no, no, I'm not doing it."

Sandra walked right up to Libby and slapped her in the face. That snapped Libby's attention. "Do you want to be responsible for the death of my children?" Sandra said.

She stared hard at Libby, making clear the question was not rhetorical. Finally, Libby managed to shake her head.

"Then get in our car."

Sandra did not wait to see if Libby followed as she stomped off down the road. Max got in behind Sandra, also not looking back. But he could hear Libby's footsteps coming along.

Chapter 24

TOWARD THE NORTHERN SIDE of Winston-Salem, just off Route 52, Max pulled into Denny's — one of the only places that never closed. Of course, there was Waffle House, but though he had lived in North Carolina for nearly a decade, some Southern traditions Max had yet to adopt. Despite having only a few customers, the thick aroma of bacon, eggs, pancakes, and coffee engulfed every inch of the diner. The soft clink of silverware, dishes, and thick mugs created a gentle background tune that always felt familiar.

The group stayed quiet until seated in a booth and served hot coffee. The waitress, an older lady with puffy, red-dyed hair, pulled out a pad and pencil, but Sandra shook her head. "Not yet," she said. Without so much as a nod, the waitress turned away.

As the caffeine flooded through Max's system, he turned his eyes upon Libby. For her part, she had regained some composure during the drive. Max suspected that given another day or two, the poor gal would have a complete nervous breakdown. After all, not only did she have to deal with witchcraft and spirits and the Brotherhood — the types of things she had tried to escape from years ago — she had also witnessed the murder of two people. People she knew.

Sandra must have been thinking along the same lines because she reached across the table and took Libby by the hand. "I know this night has been terrible. I know you want to bury yourself under the covers and forget as much as you can. But listen to me. I was not lying — the lives of our two boys are in jeopardy. So we don't have time for you to get all weepy again. Understand? Ten minutes. That's all you have. Let's hear it."

Libby stared at her mug, several long strands of her black hair dipping into the coffee. Her shoulders raised and lowered with each breath — her exhalations shivering. Perhaps Sandra had pushed too hard. Perhaps Libby's breakdown had already begun.

But when she lifted her head, Max could see that she had compartmentalized all her emotions. Every terrifying thought and horrifying memory had been locked away. It was a flimsy door that held those things, but it would last the next ten minutes.

With a voice scratchy from wailing, she said, "After you finished the Darian case with me, I wanted nothing to do with this world. You people — all of this craziness tonight — I wanted nothing like that ever again. For the last five years, I've managed to stay away from it all. I may have read a book or two on the subject now and then. I watched a couple cheesy ghost hunter shows. But the thought of actually going out at night on a case never crossed my mind. Not seriously, anyway. Besides, I had a job, a boyfriend, and a life to build. Huh, already I'm saying that in the past tense. I don't know if I have those things anymore."

"What got you back into it all?" Max asked.

"About two months ago, I met Angie and Gene. They had been dabbling in paranormal investigations for a few years, and they came to me because they had a problem. First question out of my mouth — why me? Apparently, one of my old friends in the business pointed them my way. He said he would've taken the case himself, but his plate was full. More likely, he hoped to lure me back in."

Sandra said, "Why would he do that? You clearly were done with it."

"Not all people are nice. Most that I've ever come across are pretty selfish. Maybe knowing that I left meant that others could leave too and he didn't like what that would mean to his identity? Or maybe he had a thing for me. Who knows? Doesn't matter. Whatever the reason, he did what he did and that led to Angie and Gene standing at my door asking for help.

"This woman, Ms. Sinauer, had made them an offer for their expertise. There was a sizable amount of money and success would have given them legitimacy. Only problem was they didn't really know what they were doing. All their experiences at ghost hunting had turned up nothing. Even if they hadn't been pointed to me from my so-called friends, they knew my name — after the Darian case, a lot of people knew my name.

"They basically wanted me to oversee what they did. They were willing to cut me in for an equal third of the payment, and most importantly, they wanted my help negotiating terms."

Max said, "So you did it for the money?"

"Thirty thousand dollars total. A third of that for one night's work — a night in which I wouldn't have to do much but oversee. You bet I did it. I needed the money. Still do. Somehow, I don't think Ms. Sinauer is going to pay me now."

"You didn't get any payment up front?"

Clacking her coffee cup as she set it down hard, Libby said, "You only gave me ten minutes. Stop interrupting. Look, the point is that they came to me and needed my help. I needed the money. But more than that, I invited them in to chat because I was hoping it would just drive it out of me. Like reading the books or watching the shows. But it became evident real fast that they did not know enough about what they were getting into. I mean they suggested I could help negotiate terms, but they had no intention of making a formal contract. Real amateur stuff. Gene had a huge amount of equipment, but when they explained to me their set up, I knew they were in trouble. They didn't know how to cover an area properly, how to record on multiple visual and auditory levels, any of it. In hindsight, I'm sure Ms. Sinauer targeted these two *because* they didn't know enough to stay out of such a questionable deal. Nobody pays money like that for what we do. Heck, people rarely pay anything at all.

"At the time, though, I thought *why not?* One night, ten grand, and I would never do it again. On top of all that, when I heard Ms. Sinauer's pitch, I thought the whole thing was fake anyway. She claimed to be a powerful sorceress of the great Brotherhood of the Rising and wanted her greatness to be documented. I thought that at best, I would be able to make a show on fraud and its perpetrators. Yet, in the back of my mind, part of me thought that if any of what Ms. Sinauer said turned out to be true — well, that's the stuff that makes a career."

Max said, "Not that you wanted to get back into this."

She looked into her coffee. "I don't know what I wanted. I think part of me expected Ms. Sinauer to summon a ghost, chat for a little bit, and send the thing back. Instead, she and her Brotherhood — well, that is, after we set everything up, they arrived with three hogs. I've got it on video. They slaughtered those poor animals for their blood and used it to call up the spirit. Have you ever heard a hog killed? They scream. Terrible sound. It'll haunt you. I know it'll haunt me."

Max shifted in the booth to face Sandra. "Is that normal?"

"Screaming hogs?" Sandra asked.

"The sacrifice. I thought you had to use human blood for blood magic."

Sandra waved off the red-headed waitress for a second time. "They're not using blood magic — not the formal, witchcraft kind. If they're using a real practice that predates witchcraft, I suppose sacrificing a pig could work. After all, even the Bible has animals being sacrificed all the time."

Libby said, "The Bible — that's what I was thinking. When they were killing the hogs, I thought that it was like something out of the Bible. Only they had a hokey element to it. It felt put on — like a bad stage production. I really thought it was still a fraud at that point.

"But as they went through their ceremony, strange things began to happen. The air started humming as if strained under a great stress and that it might even crack open. Lights blinked on and off. All the candles went out. We recorded everything, and I thought it was over. I actually thought that was the whole experience we had come to witness.

"Then Ms. Sinauer said it was time to bring up the vessels, and I knew she meant me, Angie, and Gene. I remember pushing back my chair and taking a few steps toward the door. We had the time it would take them to get to our operations room. We could've escaped. I was about to suggest we run for it, but then Mr. Carroll spoke up. He had been there as more an observer than a participant. At least, that's how I saw him. But through the monitors, we watched as he began arguing — complaining is more like it. He was fuming. They had promised him an opportunity to join the Brotherhood, and this spirit being put in the proper vessel was to be his test. Yet now Ms. Sinauer wanted to use me and the others as vessels. He yelled that splitting the spirit in three vessels would weaken it and what's the point if it doesn't have its strength.

"Those two continued to shout at each other, but I don't know what they said after because by that point, I had heard enough. I told Angie and Gene to gather their things. We were leaving. Gene sent everything we had recorded onto the server, and Angie tried to remove the hard drive. But we were too late. Those two big guys showed up and grabbed us.

"They drove us to a house — I don't know where we were — and they treated us well enough as far as being held hostage goes. Whenever we asked questions about what was going on, they ignored us, so I don't know much more. Around three in the morning, they woke us up, showed us into the car, and drove us back here. You saw the rest."

Libby tried to pick up her coffee mug, but her shaking hand only clattered the mug against the table. She sniffled and managed another wobbling breath.

"I'm sorry any of this happened to you," Sandra said. "I wish I could tell you it's over, but Ms. Sinauer is still out there. So is the rest of the Brotherhood. While I can't force you to do anything, I strongly suggest you get out of town. Go back to your old life. That boyfriend is probably still waiting for you, your job is still there, your life is still there. Don't tell us where you're going, just go."

Max said, "Listen to my wife. She's smart. We don't have a

lot of money, but I did slash your tires and that means you can't ever get that car back. Not without the Brotherhood knowing. So, once you get settled, you contact us, and we'll pay whatever we can to help out. If you want us to drive you someplace right now, we can do that, too. There's a bus stop not far up the road from here."

After spending the last minutes delving into unsettling memories, the practicality of Max and Sandra's words hit Libby with visible force. She popped to her feet as if the booth had scalded her. She looked back at them. "If you really want to help me, forget me." She walked away.

Max flopped back and drank as much of the coffee as he could before burning his tongue. "I know she did her best, but I feel like we needed more information."

"I think we got quite a lot. In fact, she gave me a bit of a crazy idea."

"Am I supposed to like the sound of that? Because I don't."

Sandra sipped her coffee. "You're supposed to trust me."

"That I do."

"Good. Because we've got Mr. Carroll's book from the Brotherhood. That has a lot of information in it. I think between that and my witchcraft resources, I should be able to find one or two spells that might help us. If I can figure out how to bring them together into one spell, maybe it'll work."

"You really think so? I'm not doubting you, but sometimes you're telling me that you're just a beginner and have a lot to learn, and other times you seem to be a heck of a lot more powerful than I'm realizing."

"I've had a very unorthodox tutelage. Most beginning witches don't learn their craft while facing off against the likes of Mother Hope or Grandma Mobley or any of the others we've had to deal with. So, even though I'm missing a lot of the foundational basics — and I'm trying to learn those as fast as possible — I do know some high-level things, too."

Max dug out his wallet and placed a few bills on the table. "Okay, then. I'll drive you back to the office so you can work. Then I'll go get Irene and Mr. Carroll and bring them back. If we're lucky, Mr. Carroll will brag about how brilliant he is and let slip a few more key details that'll help you."

As they crossed the parking lot to the car, they found Libby leaning on the bumper.

"I can't leave," she said with a defeated whisper. "Angie and Gene are dead because I didn't have the sense to stop them from being greedy. Because I was greedy. I'm responsible for that."

Sandra said, "It's not your fault. They would've gone without you."

"Doesn't matter. It's what I feel. And I'm not leaving Winston-Salem or North Carolina until I see that they get justice. You said I have a life to go back to, but I don't. Not until I settle things here."

"You sure this is what you want?"

"You made it seem like time was a factor. Do you want to keep questioning me?"

Max unlocked the car. "Get in."

Chapter 25

CRAWLING UP ADA AVENUE, Max knew trouble had come to Mr. Carroll's house. The front door stood wide open and the screen door had been ripped right off the hinges. Max parked on the side of the road. He stared at the house for a full minute, waiting for somebody to come running out.

But the place remained silent. If people were still in there, the sound would be evident in the late night air.

Best to be safe, though. He pulled out his handgun. As he skirted by the chain link fence and across the lawn, he wondered how long he would continue to carry an unloaded weapon. Bluffing with it had become a comfortable habit — even if a bit ineffective. But someday, he would probably need bullets.

He hoped that moment would not be now.

The closer he came to the house, the faster his pulse raced. He worried that his heart couldn't take the cycle of tension that he had been looping through all night long. Drug addicts probably felt the same way. Highs and crashes, highs and crashes. Only it had gone on so long this night, he couldn't tell one from the other. He knew only that his blood pumped hard, his skin prickled while breaking into a sweat, and his mind juggled too many problems.

He pressed up against the house before peeking through the open doorway. The place had been ransacked. Torn to pieces.

Max stepped into the living room as if afraid he might wake some dangerous animal. When he had left, Mr. Carroll had been bound to a chair — that chair now lay in pieces on the floor and couch. Somebody had smashed it against the wall. In fact, that person must have smashed the chair several times at several locations — numerous holes in the drywall revealed pink insulation. But as much as things had been destroyed, it did not look as if somebody came searching for a small object — there were plenty of books still on shelves and drawers unopened. This looked like something else. A struggle, perhaps.

Standing in the middle of the living room, feeling the dread of another terrible event mounting on this night's ever-growing pile, he called out, "Irene?"

No answer.

"Irene? You here?"

He heard a dull thump from the kitchen. Moving fast now, Max entered the kitchen as the pantry closet opened. Irene stepped out like a teenager afraid she got caught drinking. Until she saw Max. Then her apprehension vanished, her attention lifted, and her cheeks puffed as she blew out a long breath.

"You okay?" he asked.

"I thought they'd come back, that Mr. Carroll had betrayed me."

"Why would you worry he would betray you? He already did. Betrayed us all. Where is he? Did the Brotherhood do this? What's going on?"

With a gentle push, Irene walked by Max and headed down the hall. "Come on. This way."

She led him to Mr. Carroll's bedroom — cramped, off-white walls, dominated by a queen-size bed with crisp sheets and a burgundy pillow. Irene sat on the corner of the bed.

"There are a lot of bad things you could say about Mr. Carroll," she said. "You've probably already said most of them in your head and a good number of them out loud. But I noticed something about this man, and after you and Sandra left, I confirmed it. Mr. Carroll believes himself to be a true Southern gentleman. Now, I know our Southern heritage has some horrible blemishes. Terrible things that will take a long time to rectify — if we can ever get over ourselves enough to admit to half of it. However, there are some admirable qualities about our culture, as well. And the gentleman side of being a Southern gentleman is one of them."

Max's adrenaline still pumped hard making it difficult to stand still and listen. Though she rambled, he had met enough people like this to know to keep his mouth shut. She had a point, and if he could find his patience, she would get to it sooner than if he interrupted. For once, he managed to fight back his urge to speak and instead simply let Irene get out what she needed to get out.

Gesturing at his hands, Irene said, "You can stop fidgeting. I know our situation. I'll be as quick as I can. Now, Mr. Carroll and I chatted for a while, and I think he thought he was buttering me up. But I saw through that. However, as I stated, I also saw a true gentlemen. Because at one point his phone rang. I fished it out of his back pocket — which he was properly embarrassed about — and saw the call came from Ms. Sinauer. He told me who she was, I assume you know, and he warned me that she would be fixin' to kill him. He told me I should hide. That was it. He did not ask me to set him free nor did he suggest I stay and become a victim. He understood that I would not leave my guard of him, so his best solution was that I hide."

She took a lengthy pause, and Max guessed that she had finished her summary. He said, "I'm thankful you're okay."

"I am as well."

"Did you see who came in here? Did they kill Mr. Carroll?"

"I did as Mr. Carroll suggested. Hid in the pantry. He promised they would not come in there, that they only wanted him, and that he would secure my safety by giving himself to them. I did not see who came, although I heard both a man's voice and a woman's. I heard them smashing up the place, but he told them to stop. That you had tied him up and ran off for the warehouse. They did not kill him. I would've heard that. Plus, you would've noticed a heck of a lot of blood all over the living room, and you haven't mentioned that."

"Okay — for the moment we can assume Mr. Carroll's alive. Or on his way to his death. Either way, that's not our priority. Saving Drummond is everything right now."

"Then this will help." Irene reached under the bed and

pulled out a thin book. "Mr. Carroll is not a fan of Ms. Sinauer. Though he does not necessarily want to help us, I think he felt a bit of that old adage — *enemy of my enemy*. Or perhaps he didn't want to see a sweet Southern lady like myself come to any harm."

Max cocked his head to look at the book. It had a flaky, white cover as if made from albino eel skins, and in the center, a pentagon with a star in it had been drawn. "You open it up yet?"

"Of course. It's more about the Brotherhood. Specifically, this is a collection of the spells they had uncovered over the centuries."

"Looks awfully thin for that?"

"Without witchcraft or access to a witch's books, magic can be very difficult to learn anything about."

"Let's get this book to Sandra. There's got to be something in there that can help." He reached over, but Irene pulled it away.

"Mr. Carroll told me two important things. He told me about a specific spell in this book. One designed for someone like me — a psychic. He also told me that whatever way we attempt to gain control of the spirit, we will fail unless we know the spirit's name."

Max had quietly been building a new image of Mr. Carroll, one in which he was still a power-hungry madman but also the version of a Southern gentleman that Irene had painted. But now Max saw the worst kind of used car salesman. "He wouldn't tell you the name, would he?"

"I think he's trying to buy time for himself. The more I recall what I heard, the more I think it was a show. Somebody freed him, but all that violence I heard — I'm not so sure what to believe."

"You think he's lying about needing the spirit's name?"

"Not at all. But he's a calculating man. When he told me that with the spell in this book, I can more easily make contact with the spirit, I grew suspicious of his motives."

"Doesn't matter what his plan is, if he even has one — not

right now. We lose everything if we don't get Drummond. So, if that spell gets the spirit's name, we need to get it. If you can bring that thing here, then why are we —"

"Not like that. It won't actually be here. I'm a psychic — I communicate with the dead. I can't summon them to physical form. With this spell, I can make contact. A connection. With that, we can talk to the spirit. If we can learn its name, we can control it as if we held its totem."

"Then we get Drummond back."

"Maybe."

Max did not like any of this. His gut told him to doubt everything Mr. Carroll had said and go to the library to research in-depth. With Sandra at his side, they could analyze and dissect this book until they found the truth. If it turned out that Mr. Carroll spoke honestly, they would be able to form an intelligent plan of attack.

Yet he could practically hear Drummond floating behind him, clicking his tongue, and shaking his head. The ghost would say that he did not like the feel of this either, but with time being a factor and the boys' lives at risk, might as well jump in and force the spirit's hand.

I really miss you, pal.

"Okay," Max said, ignoring the gymnastics competition twirling his stomach. "Let's do it."

"Now? Here?"

"Now. Here."

Chapter 26

THEY NEEDED FLOOR SPACE, and without a word spoken between them, they opted to avoid the living room. Instead, Max tilted the mattress against the wall followed by the box spring. Mr. Carroll had only a basic metal bedframe which disassembled with ease. As Max cleared these things away, Irene hastened into the kitchen and returned with a thick, red candle. She squatted in the middle of the floor, lit the wick, and opened the book. "Shut the lights, please."

Max obliged, and the red glow gave the room a garish sheen. Irene wafted the candle fumes towards her face with gentle hand motions like a rabbi preparing to pray. She paused to check the book once more.

"This will take a little time," she said. "It's not like I'm walking into a room where there is a spirit and I'm trying to communicate with it. Here, I'm focusing my psychic energy to reach out and find the spirit. Kind of like radio waves, I guess."

"Are you trying to say I should leave you alone?"

"Give the boy a medal. I'll call you when I'm ready."

Max meandered down the hall and into the living room. He thought about cleaning things up, but the idea of expending that much energy did not sit well. Whatever reserves he maintained, he would need soon enough. He hoped.

He collapsed on the couch, his head resting back. It would be so easy to close his eyes. No. He sat forward and dug out his phone. Sliding his finger through photos of Sandra and the boys, he shook his head. They were crazy. Simple as that.

From now on, he should decline any jobs that sounded simple. They never were. In fact, he wouldn't be surprised if it turned out that all the cases which appeared simple in the beginning had turned out to be the ones that nearly killed them off — every single time.

Maybe I shouldn't be taking any cases that jeopardize our lives.

Because now that he considered his situation, he had to admit that the Sandwich Boys would not be in trouble right now if Max and Sandra had never taken the case to start. Drummond would not be fighting for his ghostly life right now. Perhaps all of Max's anxiety and uncertainty over the boys and Drummond was simply his brain's way of sending a message — *it's time to end this. Close the agency.* That was the thought that kept trying to break through his consciousness yet never found the chance.

And here it was.

He and Sandra had talked about it before. His sleep deprived brain thought they may have even spoken about it that evening. Or maybe he simply thought about it. *Or maybe I'm thinking about it now.*

He slapped his cheeks and gave his body a shake. He had to stay clearheaded. Stay awake.

Drummond had told him of similar moments of doubt in the old ghost's past. "Plenty of times I've thought about hanging up my hat," Drummond had said. "There will always be cases that stand out, that shake your beliefs, that make you wonder if what you're doing is worth it. Cases that threaten you or your loved ones, cases that bring you to the brink of death. And you stop in the middle of it all and think to yourself — *why am I doing this?* You really question it to the core."

"What's the answer?" Max had asked.

"I don't think there is one answer. It's different for different people."

"For you?"

"Somebody had to do the job, and I knew I could do it well. When I finished a case, even a tough one, I felt like I actually helped somebody. Oftentimes, I helped the person who hired me and I also helped the ghost. Because, usually, the ghost simply needs to know how to move on."

"You didn't move on."

"That should tell you something. I believe in what I'm doing so strongly that I've stayed back here. Plus, I care about you guys."

Max trusted every word, but he also knew something more drove Drummond to keep fighting. The undeniable fact — this path never ended. Dealing with these kinds of cases had an attraction, an addictive quality, and the high felt when successful kept the agency from ever folding.

The full truth — Max and Sandra had faced death many times already. They had faced those deaths with and without the boys. Of course, they didn't want to put anybody in harm's way, but the idea of life without the Porter Agency grated like bone against bone.

Besides, though he might argue that quitting would protect the boys, he did not believe it. Closing the Agency meant nobody was there to stop the witches, the Hulls, and now the Brotherhood. Maybe somebody would come along eventually to pick up the fight, but as Drummond had said, Max knew the Porter Agency could handle these things the best of anybody. Seemed to him that quitting created more dangers than going forward.

Irene's soft voice drifted down the hall. "I'm ready."

Approaching the bedroom, the deep red candlelight played against the corridor wall. Max's throat tightened. He could smell the candle burning, and the walls felt closer together. His mouth dried.

When he entered the room, Irene sat like the statue of a meditating woman. The candle beneath her cast shadows upward, freezing her face like a kabuki mask. She hummed a steady soft note.

Max moved back into the doorway. He did not want to break her train of thought, but he also did not want to get too close. Everything appeared fine, yet his body fired warning signals throughout his system.

As the humming continued, Irene sprinkled something over the flame. Little sparks crackled. When she placed her hand in her lap, the flame on the candle rose high. It weaved in the air like a snake summoned by a charmer. The flame brightened, flashed like a camera, and then shifted hue into a dark red.

"It's coming," she whispered.

The crimson flame continued to darken until it became a rich plum. This strange-colored lick of fire reduced little by little until it reached a normal size. But it did not stop there. It lowered beneath the wick until it sputtered out.

With no other light source, Max expected to be in a dark room. But the familiar purple sphere hovered in the air above the candle. With its horrible, gravel voice, it said, "Not you."

Irene lifted her head to stare directly at the inhuman spirit. "You don't belong here. This is not your realm."

The inhuman spirit hollered. Cracks formed along the wall and across the ceiling. Max could feel the bumps beneath the floor even as he heard them coming through the walls. When the mini-earthquake settled, Irene stood on firm legs.

"You do not scare me. And you cannot harm me. I have my faith and I am the one who called you here. So I will be the one to send you back. Go. Begone to your home. You are not welcome here."

The purple glow shifted from side to side as if shaking its head. Irene may have called it to Mr. Carroll's house — *and this was only a psychic connection, sheesh* — but she had not summoned it from wherever it came. She had no control over it, and they both knew it.

The spirit darted forward at Irene, but she did not budge. It split around her as she called its bluff. When its two halves reconnected behind her, they looked back and Max could see its surprise. It did not realize another was in the room.

Now that Max had gained its attention, he recognized the big problem in their plan. Irene had her faith with her at all times. It was her religious belief, and it lived within her. But Max's faith, his strength that fought off this inhuman spirit, came from having Sandra at his side. And she wasn't there.

The spirit had drawn the same conclusion and wasted no time charging at Max like a purple bull in an arena hungry to devour the matador.

Chapter 27

CHOP. CHOP. CHOP.

The sound swam around Max's head like a nun with a ruler smacking her hand. Except Max had never been to Catholic school. He had never known any nuns. He wasn't even Catholic.

Chop. Chop. Chop.

He knew that sound, though. It called to him as if it were his name. He wanted to move towards it.

How could he? He couldn't even see.

Then open your eyes, idiot, he thought.

With the grogginess of waking from a dream, he squinted his eyes open. He stood in a hallway bathed in red. A long hallway. Endless.

Chop. Chop. Chop.

His father, of course. He knew that. Max figured he knew it the moment he had first heard the sound. As he walked down the hall, the sound grew louder and more distinct. He knew what that meant as well.

Definitely his father doing the chopping. And the chopping meant ...

The hall ended in an open field. Bathed in moonlight, the dead rows of torn up corn ended near the edge of a forest. His father stood there, hunched as he methodically brought his ax over and down, over and down, over and down.

Chop. Chop. Chop.

He wore no shirt, had it tied around his waist, and his exertions glistened sweat on his back. Max watched the man work and thought how wonderful it would be if time could stop. If this moment could freeze. Just him and his father, chopping wood, with nothing to concern them.

But then his father pulled the ax up, and Max saw all the blood. Of course there was blood. What else did he expect?

Coating the ax head, the ax handle, his father's hands and arms and face. The closer Max looked, the more blood he saw — on the grass, in the dirt, on the stems of cornstalks. He didn't want to look further, but he could not stop his feet from moving in.

His father chopped Irene.

"Don't get squeamish on me," his father said with a pure North Carolina accent as if he had been born in Winston-Salem instead of Detroit. "I know you don't like me. That's okay. I don't like you much, either."

It's the inhuman spirit, Max reminded himself. *It feeds off negative energy.*

"Pay attention," his father said with such parental authority that Max obeyed. "You think I want to be out here? Especially with you? Life isn't easy for either of us. But I've always had dreams, things I wanted to accomplish. A real man can't hide from those things. When you hear the call, you have to answer."

Max struggled to understand what his father said. He comprehended the words, but not the reason for them. Or perhaps the chopping of dead Irene distracted too much.

"There you go again," his father said, snapping his fingers in front of Max's face. "Things get tough and you want to hide away. That's why you never had your dreams made. You hide away in your thoughts, you hide away in books, and you lose so much living that life just happens to you instead of you doing something about it."

"You don't know what you're talking about," Max said.

This wasn't his father. This wasn't even a human being. He tried to remember that fact but found it difficult to deny something his senses assured him stood only feet away.

"Really? I'm the one who doesn't know anything?"

"I mean, sure, this is not the life I ever expected to have, but that doesn't mean it's not a meaningful life. A good life. I've got a wonderful wife and two kids and —"

"Those kids ain't yours. Not for real. And how well do you really get along with your wife?"

"I love her. You wouldn't know the first thing about it, anyway. You left."

"Can't say I left much behind."

"We didn't miss you, either. I don't care what you think of what I have, I know I've done well. Got my own business, for crying out loud."

"Do you? Drummond is the one who does all the heavy lifting while you hide away in a library. I've gotten to know him quite well in here, and from where I'm standing, it's all very clear to me. You are not necessary. The boys don't need you — they got your mother and your wife. Your wife don't need you — she's got the boys, and she can see all the ghosts including Drummond. She's become a pretty powerful witch, too. I think she can run the whole place by herself. Drummond certainly doesn't need you — he's got eternity ahead of him. In fact, I'd say I'm the only one that does need you. Or wants you, for that matter."

On one level, Max knew he should stumble back against the horrible things his father had said. However, on another level — an odd, analytical level he never knew existed — his father's words did not sting. They did not bite or poke festering wounds or do any damage at all. In fact, they made a bizarre kind of sense.

His father resumed chopping, adding a hefty grunt as he brought the ax down each time. Sounding like an exhausted workhorse forced to keep moving, he remained focused on his chopping, never peering back at Max. It was as if the conversation had been declared over.

But Max had more to say. More to think. He wanted more out of this.

An old voice spoke up. "You're letting him get in your head."

Off to the right, in the distance, he saw a pale ghost wearing a long coat and a Fedora — Marshall Drummond. Max opened his mouth, ready to burst with excitement, but even at this distance he noticed Drummond's warning expression.

"Keep that spirit busy. Keep him chopping and he won't hear me. As long as I don't get any closer. You can hear me, right?"

Max nodded — a slight movement, nothing he thought anybody would notice if they weren't looking for it.

"I'm fighting all I can against this thing. If you can see me — if you can see your old pal Drummond afloat in front of you, then I might be winning more than I thought. But the moment you two are done with your little chat, he and I are going right back at it. If I try to make a run for it, he'll have me. Now, I'm assuming you're trying to get me out."

Max nodded as before. But he couldn't help smiling ever so slightly.

His father snapped to attention. "What's so funny?"

"Nothing," Max said.

"Don't get cute with me. Just because I was gone for most of your life don't mean I can't still whoop your butt with a belt if I have to. You get it in your head right now — you're worthless. Out there with your friends, with your wife, you ain't got nothing. You want some real power? You want to actually achieve something? Open yourself up to me. Hear what I have to say. I can give you everything."

Before Max could respond, the man returned to his bloody task. Max snatched a peek at Drummond. The ghost had vanished.

No. Wait. He could see a faint outline of Drummond. The longer Max's father worked at slamming that ax into Irene's corpse, the clearer Drummond became.

Only a few seconds later, he heard Drummond. "Don't give yourself away again. It's taking a lot for me to keep coming back here. Listen, I think I know something that might help you. I want you to —"

"What you looking at over there?" Max's father gazed off toward Drummond. But the ghost had disappeared.

Max rushed over to the leftovers of Irene. He hoped to haul

his father's attention away, and to that point, he succeeded. But he also got a full view of the gore that soaked the soil. Vomit raced up his throat and he stepped away but nothing came out.

"So weak," his father said.

When Max could breathe again, he turned back to find his father studying the blood on the ground like an archaeologist over a precious find. In the distance, Max spotted Drummond once more. The ghost had a frustrated tightness to his face, and he pulled his hat down low. Holding the ends of his closed long coat, he hesitated.

Though Max could not hear Drummond anymore, he could see the ghost mouth the words — *this better be worth it.*

Drummond pulled open his coat to reveal that he wore a pink, college sweatshirt. The kind of thing a sorority girl would wear. He looked off to the side so as to avoid any eye contact. Max read the sweater — *Delta Psi Epsilon.*

The moment Max thought the Greek letters, Drummond faded into the air. Max had no clue why Drummond would show him these letters, but it must have been important. *Delta Psi Epsilon.* He would not forget.

Straightening, his father stretched his arms before picking up the ax once more. He walked over to Max. "I'm sorry if I rattled you. I want you to understand that as a father, sometimes you have to do an ugly thing or two. You have to be a man and not worry about the soft little feelings of a boy. You understand?" He gripped the neck of the ax and offered the handle. "Go on. Take it."

Max put his hands in his pockets.

"Don't be like that. Haven't you been listening? You got dreams, right? Things you want to accomplish in your life. I know how important these things are to you. A real family — that's what you've always wanted. I screwed that up for you when you were a kid, but you can have it now."

"I have a real family now."

"No, no. What you got is a real substitute family. But those kids ain't your flesh and blood. The only reason you got those boys is because they weaseled their way into your life. And that wife of yours — she never wanted you. Face the truth. You'd be better off without them all. You get rid of them and you'd have room to find someone who really loves you and wants to provide you with the things you need. Give you the dreams you seek. That's what this is for. This ax is a tool to cut your way out of the hole you're in."

Everything his father said fogged his brain like a poison gas. He understood the words, they were simple enough, yet each one when put together produced vile thoughts. Ideas Max did not agree with. Still, he could feel his hands squirming in his pockets, itching to get out and grab hold of that ax. Why? Was there something actually inside him that thought the way his father suggested?

"Come on, now." His father gave the ax a little shake. "Not much to it. You don't have to hide from being who you are deep down. I understand. I know I'm not perfect. But I'm honest. Can you be the same? Can't you admit that those boys and your wife and this crazy Porter Agency — will you admit that all those things have nothing to do with your true dreams in life? Those dreams you had when you were going off to college. Dreams of creating something new, finding the perfect woman, the perfect life. You can have it all. I want to give it to you. Son."

Max noticed that his hands were out of his pockets. One of them reached forward. It moved as if it belonged to somebody else, and Max watched it as if observing a newly discovered insect.

But then a little thought plinked in his head. "I may not have the life I dreamed of, but it's become my dream. I want the one I have now."

"Max?" The voice drifted across the fields behind him. He knew that voice — Irene. Hearing the woman he had seen chopped into pieces flooded his system with the fact that he was not in reality. Memories of those who he loved and the reason he had stepped into this nightmare washed over him.

Like a vampire facing a cross, his father hissed and high-tailed off into the forest. Max felt a hand on his arm. He looked down and found Irene giving him a gentle shake.

He stood at the edge of a forest, but it was dark. And no cornfield. A few feet away ran a local road. Further on, small homes similar to the one owned by Mr. Carroll.

"Are you okay? Can you hear me?" Irene said, her intense concern like an EMT speaking to the victim of a bad car accident.

As reality sank into his brain, he stepped in towards Irene and wrapped her in a thick hug. "You're alive. I'm so glad you're alive."

Muffled by his arms, she said, "I'm usually happy about it, too."

He chuckled as he let her go. "How long have I been out here?"

"We just got here. The inhuman spirit slammed into you, then you walked straight out here. I don't know how it did anything. I swear I only have the psychic ability. The spirit should never have been able to touch you physically. It makes no sense."

"Maybe Mr. Carroll's spell boosted more than just your psychic-ness. Or maybe the spirit honed in on your signal once you made contact."

"Possibly — the latter, not the former."

"Either way, I don't think you should try to contact it again."

"No argument here. Besides which, I doubt the spirit will follow my connection a second time. It's smart. It'll assume we've prepared some kind of trap for it."

Gesturing to their surroundings, Max said, "Looks to me like I'm the one who got trapped."

"You were never in serious danger. I've been following you, making sure nothing hit you and that you didn't do anything stupid. Kind of felt like I was dealing with a sleepwalker."

"Why did you wake me, then?"

She pointed off to the right. "When you stopped walking, I thought I saw — over there — I thought I saw Drummond."

"You saw him?"

"I don't know. I saw something, and it reminded me of him. I didn't mean to grab your arm, but I did so without thinking. Then you said his name. That's when I called out to you."

Moving with an anxious stride, Max said, "We've got to go. Drummond is still with us, and he's trying to help. We've got to get to Sandra."

"How is he helping us? What did he say?"

"Delta Psi Epsilon."

He continued on the way to his car. From further back, he heard Irene rushing to catch up.

Breathing hard, she said, "What does that mean?"

Max grinned from the corner of his mouth. "No idea. But we're going to find out."

Chapter 28

MAX SLIPPED INTO THE CITY without any trouble and snagged a parking space one block down from the office. As he and Irene hoofed up to Trade Street, he could smell the corner bagel shop prepping for breakfast. Normally, that smell would whet his appetite for the start of another day. But his stomach soured at the thought that dawn approached.

Picking up his pace, they reached the office building, zipped upstairs, down the hall, and entered the Porter Agency. A rich coffee aroma permeated the air as he walked across the lounge area toward the back of the single large room. Sandra had the rug in the lounge pulled away to reveal the casting circle he and PB had carved into the wood floor. She rested on the couch with her laptop propped on her chest as she worked. Their desks filled up the back end of the room. And, of course, the built-in bookshelf loomed over it all — Drummond's home.

Max stared at the bookshelf. He could not tell if it truly felt empty without the ghost or if it was merely his imagination.

"I know," Sandra said. "I felt it, too."

As Irene settled on the end of the couch, Max turned towards them. "I think we found something important that might help you."

He heard the toilet flush and the sink run. The restroom door opened and Libby entered. She trembled a smile. Max tossed a quizzical look at Irene. Sandra did not catch any of it — her eyes shined with excitement as she set her laptop aside.

Sweeping her feet to the floor, she rushed over to hug Max. "I'm glad you found something, but you need to hear what I've got. I think I've figured out a way to get Drummond back."

"That's wonderful. Tell me."

Bouncing around the room with the energy of a schoolgirl recounting a wonderful party, she said, "I went through several of the grimoires we've accumulated from all the covens, and I went through the witch network on the darkweb. Libby helped. We've been cross-referencing everything. From what we can tell, I think there's a bit of witchcraft we can create that has an origin predating witchcraft itself. That's the kind of spell the Brotherhood must've used. My hope is that the types of spells will be related close enough. Basically, we're going to create a connection between Drummond and an object and a location that are important to him. Things that can draw him back, giving him strength, hopefully enough to tether him to us and away from the inhuman spirit."

"Tether? Like a curse?"

"Actually, yeah. Sort of. But, if I'm reading these grimoire's correctly, there are curses that have self-ending properties. Think of it like in *Sleeping Beauty* — she's put under a curse that causes her to sleep, but built into the curse is this magic kiss that will bring her back."

"I'm not going to have to kiss him, am I?"

Heading back to her computer, she said, "Don't worry. I'll make it simply the act of stopping the spirit."

"That's simple?"

"It's a two-fer. We can't save Drummond without getting rid of the spirit anyway."

"Am I getting this right? You want to curse Drummond which will tether him to a spot, breaking him from the spirit's hold. Then, when we're rid of the spirit, the curse will release him."

"Exactly. I figured for the object, we can use the flask he hides in *Moby Dick*. That's something that has been part of his life since long before his death."

Irene said, "Yes, that's a good idea. And the location is obvious. Here."

"Here?" Max said. He looked back at the bookcase. "I guess so."

"This could work." Irene's forehead wrinkled as she pointed

a finger at Sandra. "You should know that if you succeed, you will bring back the inhuman spirit along with Drummond. It won't be like when I called it. Those times, it manifested in a psychic link, mostly psychic. But this — this would be the real thing. Like we experienced in Reynolda House but stronger. It'll be loose and probably quite angry at losing its energy source."

Max settled behind his desk. "One problem at a time."

Irene turned to Sandra. "You obviously haven't performed this spell yet. Were you waiting for us, or is there something wrong?"

The joy drifted from Sandra's face. "Libby and I have gone through the book we took from Mr. Carroll's house as well as all the resources I have. We put together the ceremony, but in every version that I can find, we have to know the name of the spirit."

"That's what we were working on," Max said.

"You have it?"

Max shook his head. "Unless this spirit's name is Delta Psi Epsilon. Irene helped me connect with the spirit again — don't get that worried look, I'm all right. You can yell at me later about the risks I took, but you would've done the same thing. The good news is that I got to see Drummond briefly. He's still with us. Not doing great, but he's with us. And he showed me these Greek letters — Delta Psi Epsilon. I don't know what it means, but he wouldn't have gone to the trouble for nothing. Believe me — the way he showed me these letters, he would never have done that, if there was any other way."

Libby hurried over to Sandra's desk. "Those letters — those are Greek letters, right?"

"That's what I've been saying."

Libby hunched over the Brotherhood book Sandra had taken. "They're Greek letters. I've seen them. There was something in here with Greek letters."

She flipped through the book for a moment and stopped on a page about halfway. "This. A whole bunch of Greek letters in a column. But I thought it seemed out of place. Nothing before or after it makes any sense about it."

Irene walked over. From her bag, she pulled out the book she had found under Mr. Carroll's bed. "This is another book from the Brotherhood."

"Let me see," Libby said, snatching the book so fast, Irene never had a chance to stop her.

Sandra said, "It's okay. Let her work. In fact, Irene, I could use your help."

Max watched as Irene crossed back to Sandra, and the two crouched around the casting circle. Libby poured over the books like a desert camel finally reaching an oasis. He knew that feeling. That love of research which propelled him through night after night of books and newspapers and websites, searching for some small nugget of information.

He thought it was more than that for her, though. Most likely, she had never seen anybody murdered in front of her eyes. This was PTSD. This was her brain latching onto any normal task and using it to blot out all else. This was her soul tying a latticework wall around her in hopes that it might protect her. But there were too many holes. There always were.

He reached back to the bookcase and pulled out *Moby Dick*. Sandra had returned the flask from her purse. A row of short glasses sat on the shelf above. Max grabbed two and walked over to Libby.

"Here." He poured a couple fingers worth.

She stared up at him until he poured two more. "Thanks."

Sitting on the corner of the desk, Max said, "I'm really sorry you got caught up in all this."

She sipped the whiskey and kept her eyes on the books. "It's not your fault."

"I don't know about that. The last bunch of years, we've been focused entirely on the Hull family, and then this coven of witches called the Mobleys, and at the same time we were dealing with another group called the Magi. But this Brotherhood of the Rising has been around longer than witchcraft. Maybe we should have been paying more attention. Maybe we would've seen them earlier. If we had done that, then we would never have reached this point. You would never have been brought in on this."

"You're being selfish in your morose pity. A group like the Brotherhood doesn't last this long without knowing how to hide. Especially in plain sight. Besides, when we first met, you weren't that knowledgeable about any of this world. Even your wife hardly knew what she was doing."

She had a point. Plus, and this bothered him most of all, the Hulls did not know about the Brotherhood, either. If they had, they would have brought Max a case related to the group long ago — especially when he first moved to North Carolina, when the Hulls had complete control over magic in the state. During that time, any sign of the Brotherhood would have been a threat to Hull sovereignty. They would have brought Max in with the hope that he would solve their problems while also getting himself killed. Two birds, one stone.

He drank some of his whiskey. "We appreciate you helping out, but you should know that if it gets to be too much, then nobody will blame you if you want to leave."

"I'm not leaving." She spoke with a clear threat growling underneath.

"Okay. In that case, happy to have you."

"Then why are you talking about making me leave?"

"Nobody is making you do anything."

Libby pounded her fist on the table as she rose. "You feel responsible because you didn't know about the Brotherhood? Because while you were off fighting all these other threats, you missed one? Is that what's got you so worried that you need to come over here and try to get me to console you? Two young people died tonight because of me. Not because I missed something or went off somewhere else, but because I agreed to help them. Because, deep down, I didn't want to walk away from this life."

"I'm sorry. I didn't want to anger you. Trust me, this is important — negative emotions, negative energy attracts the inhuman spirit. We have to be careful —"

"Really? You're going to explain the obvious to me? Listen

closely. If you want to reduce the negativity in this room, then you should back off. Go sit at your desk and do nothing. Because you're pissing me off."

"Max?" Sandra's voice cut in.

Libby returned to her seat and her books. Max wanted to say something more. Instead, he heeded Sandra's call — warning, more likely.

He walked over to the casting circle. Sandra and Irene had outfitted the circle with a full five-point star within the circle and a triangle in the center of the star. Several lines of text in a language Max never hoped to learn had been written in chalk along various parts of the geometric shapes.

"We ready?" he asked.

"Almost. But we still need the name."

Glancing over his shoulder, he said, "Give her time."

"We're running out."

With a sharp noise, Libby said, "I can hear you. And I've got the name. Oxorot."

"You sure?" Sandra said.

Libby walked over and handed her a slip of paper. "Write it down."

Sandra stared at the paper as if reading an original holy text. Her hand trembled as she picked up a piece of white chalk and inscribed the name. When she finished, she set the chalk down, licked her drying lips and sat back with a sigh.

"Did it work?" Max asked.

"We haven't done it, yet." Sandra snickered before drawing in a cleansing breath. "We need to be ready for when it comes. Irene, Libby, will you please secure the room?"

Irene handed Libby a package of salt. As Max stood by his wife, Libby drew lines of salt across the doorways and windowsills. While she worked, Irene picked up a fresh piece of chalk and inscribed a symbol upon the door and on either side of the window frames.

Sandra checked over her work once more as she spoke to Max. "We need to pull in Drummond with all of our hearts, all of our positive energy. That's what's going to give him strength, help him separate from the grip of the inhuman spirit. I can't guarantee how long I can hold the spirit. I can't even guarantee this'll work at all. But there's no time left. It's six in the morning. The sun will be up in an hour."

Max held her hand. "We can't let that thing get any stronger. Not for Drummond, not for the boys, not for us, not for the whole state."

"Maybe the world," Irene said.

Max had not considered that the spirit might get that powerful — that it even could. But he did not want to find out.

"Then we do this. Now."

Chapter 29

OVER THE YEARS, Max had watched Sandra perform many spells. Some simple, some more advanced. He had never seen her attempt anything this complex.

Though the prep work had been nothing unique — time-consuming and exacting but not anything different than he had seen her do in one combination or another previously — now that they had begun the actual spell, he understood the difficulty that awaited them. Starting at the north point of the circle, Sandra lowered her head to where the star's point met the circle. Irene tiptoed to the side closet where Sandra kept much of her witchcraft paraphernalia. She returned with two black candles. When Sandra lifted her head, she accepted the candles and placed one on either side of the star's point. Remaining on her knees, she shifted to the next point and repeated the procedure, moving with precise care — any slip of her position could ruin the spell. By the time she completed her way around the circle, ten black candles with wide bases tapering to ten wicks had been carefully arranged around the five star points. Max assumed Sandra's knees ached from the hardwood floor.

Uttering a soft groan, she sat in the middle of the circle and star and triangle, lowered her head, clasped her hands together, and closed her eyes. Irene gestured for everyone to step back and give Sandra space to concentrate. "The quieter we are," Irene whispered, "the faster this should go."

Max locked his hands behind his back to keep from fidgeting. He wanted Sandra to feel as comfortable as possible, but surely she could feel the tension of Irene, Libby, and himself all staring at her. Libby, especially. Her intense scrutiny and the way her tongue and teeth could not stop touching her lips, playing with her lips, bothered Max more than anything. If the mental trauma she had suffered lashed out in any form that caused harm to come to Sandra, Drummond, or the boys, Max thought his own reaction might be equally dramatic.

With a hissing that crescendoed into a pop, all ten candles ignited. Sandra hinted at a grin as she lifted her head and put her hand out to Irene. "The flask."

Irene rushed across the room, snagged the flask, and presented it to Sandra like a knight presenting a chalice to a queen. Even bowed her head.

With a graceful motion, Sandra accepted the flask and set it at her knees. "Now, the salt."

Continuing her subservient movements, Irene softly headed to the closet and returned with a small bag of salt. She proceeded to form a circle around Sandra. With that task completed, she stepped out of the casting circle and formed another salt circle encompassing the entire project. When she finished, she set the bag on Sandra's desk.

"Thank you," Sandra said. She closed her eyes and mumbled words that Max knew he would never hear.

A strange smile rose on Libby's mouth. Max leaned closer to Irene. "If you're done helping Sandra, perhaps you should take Libby out of here."

"We can't leave," Libby said, startling Max. "Even if I wanted to, which I don't. But the spell works off of energy in the air. As the spirit works off of negative energy, the spell utilizes positive energy. You'd be better off doing what I'm doing — sending all your good thoughts to Sandra."

Max watched Libby but couldn't tell if she smiled with over-exuberance — or if she had gone mad from everything she had experienced. One thing, however, he knew — introducing negative energy into the room would be a bad idea. He had no intention of forcing anybody out.

A loud thump against the walls broke his thoughts. The ten flames surrounding Sandra stretched high into the air, momentarily obscuring her. Max held his breath until the flames settled down and he saw his wife remained unharmed.

He checked the ceiling and walls for cracks. Sandra rose to her feet and brought her hands up as if trying to feel something solid around her. Another thunderous boom, followed by three sounds that sickened Max.

Chop. Chop. Chop.

Sandra continued mumbling quietly to herself, but every so often, she punctuated her words with a loud, "Oxorot." Each time she said its name, another blast of noise reverberated through the office. Yet each time she said its name, Max caught flashes of a sphere — a glowing, purplish ball. And each time she called its name, that ball stuck around a little longer. Until, finally, it did not leave.

It hovered in the casting circle, caught between the two salt circles like a moon orbiting Sandra. Every time that ball went by Max, he could feel his father's presence. He could feel that terrifying gaze watching him, waiting for him to reach out and take hold of that ax.

This is all they allow you to do, a voice said in Max's head. A stranger's voice.

Max shut his eyes tight. He tried to drown out the voice by humming, but as soon as he began, his humming turned into sounds that mimicked the voice until the voice dominated.

This is it, Max. The ladies here are going to take over. They have no use for you. It's not a question of if but when. And I'll tell you this, when it happens, you'll have to decide how you want to go out. You can let them marginalize you until you're nothing but an insect. Sandra will realize how weak you are, she'll divorce you, she'll take the boys, she'll take the agency, heck, she'll even take Drummond. There'll be nothing left. You'll find yourself standing at the train station, heading back to Michigan with your mother. Maybe you won't even have that much.

"Shut up. Shut up," Max hissed.

Or you can believe in me. I haven't lied to you. I've been trying to get you to free yourself, to take control of your life, to follow your dreams. Instead of waiting for these vipers to minimize you into nothing, you simply have to man up. Shut them down before they have a chance to shut you down. Then, the world is yours.

Max didn't believe any of it. At least, he didn't want to believe any of it. But he could not stop part of his brain from picturing events as Oxorot had dictated them. Sandra was not the kind of person to do the things Oxorot suggested, but Max's mind pictured those things nonetheless. He couldn't stop it. The emotions that connected to those ideas swirled through his heart.

Max spun Irene towards him. "Slap me."

"What?" she said.

"Slap me. Clear my head. Get this thing out of me."

Though she did not hit him, she must have understood. She pulled him close, clutching him, and offered soft words as a mother might soothe her child. "You're going to be okay. Sandra loves you. And you love her. Together with your boys, you make an enviable family."

She continued on, and each word from her mouth vanquished a bit more of whatever plagued him.

"Look," Libby said, pointing toward the bookcase.

Drummond floated in front, more transparent than usual. He had a grim expression and did not make eye contact with anybody. He moved as if straining against chains or some other binding. But when his coat shifted, Max saw those horrible clawed hands digging into his side.

Sandra had said they needed to throw their positive energy towards him. If nothing else, Max could do that. "Hey, Drummond, do you really expect us to keep running this agency without you?"

Drummond cocked his ear to the side. He searched around, clearly unable to see Max. Irene nudged Max's arm. She wore a slim smile and gestured toward Drummond.

"Look, pal, we need you here in the office. We've got your favorite flask filled up and ready. And we've got ..." Max glanced around the office to find something, anything, to reference, but the longer he took, the dimmer Drummond became. "I don't know, partner, but I'm sure a case will come in any day now, and you know I'm only good for the research. I wouldn't be anything in the field without you. We need you."

"More," Irene said. "Don't stop. He's getting there."

Max could not tell if Irene spoke the truth or only voiced wishful thinking. Perhaps Drummond did appear more solid. Perhaps.

Glancing at his desk, Max saw a recent photo the family took at the beach. "The boys. Come on, Drummond. You don't want to miss out watching the Sandwich Boys grow up. Especially J. Now that he can see you, you've got all kinds of things you want to talk to him about. Remember? You're Uncle Drummond."

If this was working, the progress crawled. Drummond continued to look around as if lost in the dark. His confusion and frustration were only matched by his anger at fighting off the ever present claws.

Max shrugged toward Sandra. "I don't think it's going to work."

Time stood still between two seconds. Less than the flap of a hummingbird's wing, less than the beat of a heart. The world around Max stopped — long enough to see the tremors in Sandra's hands, the sweat beading on her lips, the taut cords of her neck, even the shallowness of her breath. Asking her to continue this spell was like asking a boxer with only a few years in the ring to take on the heavyweight champion.

The world continued on, spinning as fast as ever, and Sandra's eyes rolled up. As she collapsed, Max lunged across the room to catch her. He did not think about it — instinct had taken over. But in doing so, his feet swished over the salt circle and destroyed a section of the lines.

He held Sandra tight. The purple sphere shot outward across the office, and Drummond vanished. The sphere stretched like a smoky trail.

"No," Max said, wishing his words could have the magic effect of a witch.

The long snake of smoke pulled itself in to form a sphere once again. As Irene and Libby pressed against the wall, the sphere moved closer towards Max.

"Hey, Oxorot," Libby said, lurching forward with a maniacal

laugh. "You can't get out. We've salted and marked all the exits. You're stuck in here."

Max tightened his hold on Sandra. "I'm not so sure that's a good thing."

Chapter 30

MAX LOWERED OVER SANDRA, expecting a pain-soaked impact against his back at any moment. But Oxorot whooshed by him, shrieking like a beaten dog, and slammed into the wall behind. The entire office rumbled. Lifting his head, Max watched as Oxorot acted like a bowling ball, rushing across the floor and toppling everything in its way.

Max scowled. Having Sandra in his arms protected him, but that didn't protect the office.

His desk popped into the air and slammed against the bookshelf. Sparks flew from his shattered computer and all of his papers fluttered through the air. The beautiful woodwork of the built-in bookshelf splintered into shards that clattered on the ground like discarded kindling.

Irene — brave Irene — pulled a crucifix pendant from her blouse and held it before her. Its thin chain dug into the back of her neck. "I have had it with you. You are no match for my Lord. And my faith protects me. You will listen to me this time. You will obey."

Oxorot blazed through Sandra's desk, searing it like a flaming sword through paper. As sparks firecrackered off of her computer, Max couldn't stop the simple thought — *this is going to cost a fortune.*

The purple sphere reared back as it came near Libby. It stretched and deformed until it looked somewhat like the silhouette of a person. Max swore it cocked its head to the side.

"No faith," Oxorot said.

Max wanted to throw up at the leer in its voice. Irene scooped up some of the salt circle and threw it at Oxorot. The spirit immediately reverted to its spherical shape as its painful cries cracked the walls deeper. Chunks of drywall tumbled to the floor — poofing white dust into the air while exposing several studs and a tangle of wiring. Libby clutched her ears and screamed.

"There is no escape for you," Irene said. "You've had your fun. You've had your taste of our world. But you do not belong here. In the name of my Lord, I command you to return from whence you came."

Oxorot hurdled over Irene and bombed into the couch. One of the cushions flipped in the air while the spirit ripped the other two into shreds. Yellow foam spewed out. Grunting, Oxorot continued to pummel its claws through the furniture.

Libby started shaking her head. "I can't be here. I can't be here."

Max wanted to pull her in. Protect her with the same compassion that protected his wife and himself, but he knew that wouldn't work. All of Libby's positive energy had been a mask. Her terror, her trauma at what the world had thrown her way over the last twenty-four hours had taken hold of her.

"Go outside," Irene said to Libby, holding her cross toward Oxorot at all times. "Go outside and wait for us. Don't mess up the salt line."

Despite her panic, Libby was able to follow orders. Staying low as if under fire, she rushed to the office door. She opened the door slowly, careful not to disturb the salt line when the door swung inward. Then she stepped over as if avoiding a trip line. After she closed the door with equal care, Max heard her sprinting down the hallway, squealing in a mixture of delightful relief and maddened horror.

When Irene launched into another speech about her faith, her Lord, and the fact that Oxorot had to obey her, Max could see they were not going to escape this by her efforts alone. Though woozy, Sandra could lift her head now. Max eased her into a seated position.

He had an idea. Probably a bad one — but at least he would try something.

Moving fast to make sure his brain could not second guess

him into standing still, Max swiped the whiskey flask from the floor and held it over his head as he stood. "Detective Marshall Drummond, I'm calling you."

The whiskey flask warmed under his hand, and Max dared to think that this might work. Near the broken bookshelves, a blurry pale image formed. Clutching the flask tighter, Max thrust it forward as if holding a trophy for all to see.

"Come on, Drummond. Fight your way back."

A thrilling sensation coursed through his body. *Was this what Sandra felt every time she used magic?* He looked back at his wife. "It's working," he said.

But behind Sandra, on the couch, he saw the reason they were all here. The thing he had forgotten about for a mere second — Oxorot.

The spirit flew across the room, tackling Max to the floor. His wrist slammed into the hardwood, and the flask skittered into the rubble pile of his desk. Max tried to get to his knees, but Oxorot bashed him in the ribs.

Swinging his elbow back, Max hoped to catch the inhuman spirit. And he did. Except his elbow went right through the thing, and a blast of cold shot through his arm.

Then Max felt the claws. They dug in between his ribs, stinging the surface of his lungs, the excruciating ice-fire slicing through his skin. He looked down but saw no injuries. As the pain grew stronger, Max's feet left the floor. Oxorot held him in midair.

Max wanted to call for help. But Drummond was the one who could help him. He wanted to reach out towards Sandra and profess his love one last time. But the pain locked his mouth shut.

He watched Irene scurry off to the closet and gather a box of witchcraft supplies. Clutching the two Brotherhood books like babies, she handed the box to Sandra as she rushed for the door. Sandra had recovered — a little. She pulled together the ten black candles and put them in the box.

Well, at least he could be a distraction so they could escape.

But Sandra also was his strength. His faith. With a deep

breath that sent shards of frozen glass throughout his lungs, he screamed out, "Sandra, I love you!"

The claws holding Max in the air disappeared. He dropped hard to the ground, whacking his head against the floor. His tongue burned — he must have bitten it — and he spit blood.

"Honey," Sandra said, "come on."

Using Sandra's destroyed desk as a crutch, Max got his feet under him. Irene had already stepped into the hall, and Sandra stood at the door reaching out toward him. But that vile purple ball lowered between them.

"Go," Max said, the exhaustion in his voice frightening to hear.

"I'm not leaving you." Sandra had her brave mask on, but he could see the tears shimmering.

"I'll be right behind you. I promise."

Max turned away from his wife. He knew Oxorot would never let him walk by. If he was going to survive this, he needed a shield. He thought he knew where to get one.

Holding his ribs with one hand, he limped towards the bookshelves. A dim image of Drummond hovered there — possibly confused, definitely angry. Angry enough, Max hoped, to explain why Oxorot had not gone closer. It had thrown things at the bookshelves, zipped by as fast as possible, but its main aggressions had been on the opposite side of the office.

Max kept preparing himself for a blow to the back. Perhaps strong enough to crack his spine. But with each step that he took, with each foot closer to the bookshelves in which no attack came, he became more convinced that Drummond had some power left.

Sandra was right — positive energy. It gave Drummond strength.

When he finally reached the wall, Max bent down and picked up his shield. The whiskey flask. "Come on, partner. Let's get out of here."

Brandishing the flask in front of him, Max moved toward the exit. Instead of attacking, the purple ball drifted to the side, allowing Max safe passage. Could it really be that simple?

But Oxorot had no intention of giving up. It just didn't care about Max for the moment.

With staggering speed, the spirit flashed across the room and attacked Drummond. Purple claws slashed and ripped and tore at Drummond's ghostly form. All the strength that Max had given only moments earlier, all the positive power that Sandra's spell had created for Drummond, had vanished. Oxorot raged through the office and brought Drummond along.

Sandra, Irene, and Libby had left, and Max had the flask in hand, preparing to leave as well. Spirit and ghost smashed through walls and furniture and lighting fixtures — anything that could be destroyed succumbed to their path. Max did not move. He watched in hopes of finding some way to help Drummond.

A desk lamp twirled through the air, shattering against the bathroom door. All the grimoires and coveted first editions of old texts blasted across the room, their pages fluttering like ash from a forest fire.

Fire.

Max felt heat. He looked to his left. A real fire had started. It crawled up the wall, engulfing the bookshelves, devouring the books, reaching toward the ceiling. So fast.

He felt moisture on his cheek. He knew he cried, and he knew why. What more could he accomplish by standing there? If he remained, Oxorot would kill him. "Hang in there, partner. Don't give up." Afraid he might somehow catch Drummond's eye and see bitter disappointment, Max limped his way into the hall.

Chapter 31

ONCE THEY ESCAPED TO THE STREET, Max, Sandra, and Irene joined up with Libby and headed straight for the car. Black and gray smoke belched out of the second story windows behind them. In the distance, sirens could be heard approaching.

They clambered into the car, and Sandra drove off. Rounding the block, they continued west for several more blocks before parking. Then they all sat still — sweating, panting.

From the backseat, Irene scooted forward and placed a hand on Sandra. "I'm so sorry."

Though she sniffled, Sandra said, "It's only stuff. The couch, computers, the desks, all of that can be replaced."

"Not your witchcraft books," Max said. "Those grimoires — they're one-of-a-kind."

"I'm well aware. But this isn't the first time in the history of witches that fire consumed their texts, if not their lives. Why do you think researching a spell is so difficult?"

Like a child impatient from sitting in a car too long, Libby got on her knees and looked out the back window. "Is that it? Will the fire destroy Oxorot?"

"No," Irene said. "Fire won't kill it."

"Besides," Sandra added, "the only thing keeping it in the office was the salt and symbols. The fire will destroy all that. When it does, Oxorot will be free once again."

"And the skies getting light already. It's going to get very strong."

Opening and closing her grip on the steering wheel, Sandra turned her head towards Max. "I don't understand what happened. We were so close. It should have worked. It was working. You saw it, right? Drummond appeared before us."

"I don't know," Max said. "You're an incredible witch, but maybe you're not ready for this difficult a spell — if it was possible at all to begin with. But I know Drummond's the strongest fighter I've ever seen. Dawn is approaching and that'll make Oxorot stronger, but it's never faced something like Drummond. That old ghost won't give up until he has nothing left. Which means we don't give up, either. Not ever."

Sandra reached over and laced her fingers between Max's. "I know. Not just for Drummond, but for the boys. For all of us."

"Look at the bright side — now you don't have to worry about us making rent on that office."

Sandra choked out a laugh.

With a gentle pat, Irene said, "That's better. It's good that you're laughing. Although, if you need to cry, that's okay, too."

"No, we don't have time for this." Sandra put her arm over the back of the seat. "We need to figure out what went wrong, so we'll do better next time."

"Next time? Attempting this spell took everything out of you. Another time might kill you. Not to mention, that spirit assaulted your husband and burned down your office."

"Yet Drummond still needs our help."

"Risks of the job," Max said.

"We've got the candles, the salt, the Brotherhood books, the flask — what went wrong?"

They grew silent. Libby's voice, muted as she continued looking out the back window, broke in. "Not enough positive energy."

Max said, "What?"

"You said this spell worked off positive energy. That's the point of the flask, isn't it? To make a beacon out of something Drummond's attached to. If he's surrounded by Oxorot, fighting it almost nonstop, then you can think of him as being stuck in a thick fog. The flask and our positivity is the lighthouse leading him to safety. We simply weren't bright enough to shine through."

Sandra said, "But we love him."

"Guess it's not enough." Libby sat back.

Before Max could snap a comment in defense of his wife, Irene said, "She might be right. Not that we don't love Drummond enough, but that our love is not what the spell is calling for. Drummond has existed for nearly a century. He's only known the two of you for a few years and me for even less. Why should our love outweigh his entire existence?"

"I thought love was supposed to be the ultimate positive force," Max said.

"It is — psychically speaking. But the spell calls for an object and a location that matters to the lost ghost. That's a physical expression. Things so important when he was living as to draw him near. Our love might be the tipping point once he's here, but we have to get him here first. And with the fire, we've lost our —"

Max's entire demeanor shifted as his brain fired off new connections. "An object and a location — the flask and the office."

"Yes, that's what I'm trying to say."

"No, no. We have the right object — the flask. But the wrong location." He pointed to Sandra. "Our office was not where Drummond originally worked. It's not the original office. That was the place when we first moved here — the old office. The one he was bound to by a witch's curse."

Sandra started the car. The clock read 6:32 AM. "There's still time."

She pulled into the street, tires screeching as they burned down toward 4th Street.

Chapter 32

TEN MINUTES LATER, they parked in the nearby garage and hustled to the old office building — well, where the office building had been. Across the street from the YMCA, the building Drummond used as an office back in the 1930s and 40s, the same building Max and Sandra first occupied when they moved to North Carolina, had been demolished. They stared at a small parking lot nearly full with four cars and two vans sitting cold from the long night.

"Let's get started," Max said.

Sandra and Irene carted candles and chalk toward the back of the lot, trying to approximate where Drummond's office would have been located. Of course, the office had been several floors up, but every little bit would help. Plus, setting up the spell behind the cars would draw less attention.

Max pointed Libby to one corner of the lot to watch for pedestrians coming along the sidewalk. He took the opposite corner.

Libby said, "We shouldn't be doing this now. People are waking up, getting ready, going to work."

"It's been my experience that when confronted by the supernatural, most people have infinite depths of denial."

"But it's almost dawn. Oxorot is going to be much stronger. This is crazy for us to try and attack it now."

"It certainly won't be expecting us."

"But —"

"Look, we're going forward with this. We've given you plenty of outs and you've chosen to stay. It's too late now. We need you."

He hated to sound so harsh, especially considering her

fragile state, but the opportunity for second-guessing had long gone by. Libby had been right about one thing, though — they were out of time. No way could he summon up all his positive feelings if he had to spend his remaining minutes arguing with her. He couldn't tell if she understood his position, but she did not run off and she stopped her protests. Instead, she leaned against the brick wall of the neighboring building and kept her eye on the street.

Max inched back from the curb for a better look at Sandra. From what he could tell, she had already begun the spell. Another step back and he was certain. Irene stood nearby handing black candles as Sandra repeated the movement from one point of the star to the next.

Two cars drove by. Soon there would be more. A lot more.

One of the street lights flickered and went out. Probably on a timer or a light sensor. But then the entire block flickered and went out. As Max thought the words — *that doesn't seem right* — he saw the wall of flame rise from the back of the parking lot. The ten candles burned brighter than before, higher than before.

A young man in a business suit carrying a briefcase strolled by. He tripped two steps as he looked at the flames.

"Controlled burn," Max said. "Don't worry."

The man nodded as if this made perfect sense and continued on his way. A moment later, the flames died down to their normal height. Max crossed his fingers that nobody who owned one of the cars in the lot would bother to come this morning. Other than that, it appeared they had everything working fine.

"We've got trouble," Libby said.

Of course. Max stepped onto the sidewalk to get a look. Marching up toward them, he saw Ms. Sinauer and her band of lunatics. "Crap."

A purplish color painted the back of the parking lot. Max had to hope Sandra and Irene could create enough positive energy on their own because he and Libby were about to create plenty of negative.

He stepped over to Libby's side, and the two of them blocked the sidewalk. Ms. Sinauer snickered as they approached. Behind her, Punk Girl, Goatee, and Shadow postured like 1950s hoodlums readying for a rumble.

Max crossed his arms and puffed up like a bouncer. "We're not letting you through."

Ms. Sinauer raised an eyebrow. "Oh, really? You think the two of you can stop us?"

"We don't have to stop you for long. Just long enough."

"Going to run away again? We'll find you. It's not hard."

Max paused. How did they find him? If they had a witch, he would believe they cast a spell; however, their record with magic was pretty low. They probably had a much more mundane and practical approach — he would have to check over his clothes for any kind of tracking bug.

"Turn around," he said. "Go home."

"You don't really think we'll obey that, do you?"

He snatched a peek at Libby. Though she looked pale, she held her ground. He suspected it wouldn't take much for them to break her, though — unless her anger overwhelmed her traumatic memories of the Brotherhood.

Ms. Sinauer said, "Because you're too thick to recognize what's in front of you, I'll make it clear. We will do anything we need to do to get what we want. If what you saw in the warehouse wasn't evidence enough, then perhaps watching your own blood spill will bring clarity to the point."

"You talk a big game, but we defeated you with a lot of sneezing."

Goatee involuntarily rubbed his nose. Ms. Sinauer opened her mouth to say something, but her eyes glittered with purple reflections from behind Max. Her lips curled into an ugly and fierce sneer.

"That spirit belongs to us," she said. "You can't make a deal with it. We won't allow that."

"You're not stopping what we're doing."

She shoved Max back like a schoolyard bully. "What makes you think we want you to stop? Carl, get in there."

Shadow cracked his knuckles as he pushed by Max and Libby. *Doesn't look like a Carl,* Max thought. He stepped towards Carl in an attempt to block the man, but Goatee and Punk Girl rushed forward. Goatee took hold of Libby, and Punk Girl reached for Max. He slipped to the side, but she read his movement, countered with a pivot around, and wrenched his arm behind his back.

Pushing on his arm, she led Max toward the back of the parking lot. Ms. Sinauer and Carl stayed up front while Goatee and Libby brought up the rear.

More cars passed by. While Max knew there were more pedestrians, too, some instinct had most avoid this stretch of sidewalk. Those that did meander into view managed to avoid seeing anything — they suddenly checked their phones or looked at a backfiring car or found a speck of dirt floating in the air more interesting.

At the back, Sandra sat in the center of her complicated casting circle. She held Drummond's flask. Irene stood by, and when she saw Max, he said, "We didn't do so good."

Ms. Sinauer approached and Irene made a fist.

"Relax," Ms. Sinauer said. "We don't want this to stop you. In fact, we know a little trick that'll help speed the process."

Carl walked up to the edge of the salt circle. Irene inched away from his hulking body. From his belt, he pulled out a small but clearly sharp knife. Holding his free hand over the casting circle, he gave Max a sadistic wink. The man's hand had numerous scars running across the palm. It was about to get one more.

With an efficient motion, Carl sliced open his hand and then made a fist. As the drips fell into the circle, the candle flames rose higher and burned brighter. The purple sphere grew larger, and behind Sandra, the pale image of Drummond appeared.

Sandra spasmed as if receiving an electric jolt. As Carl squeezed his fist, pumping more blood into the circle, Max tried to free his arm. Punk Girl held him tight. Despite the energy smashing into her, Sandra's eyes remained closed and the spell continued.

"Stop this," Max said.

Ms. Sinauer motioned for Carl to spread more of his blood. "Don't worry about your wife. She's much too strong for the spirit to use. It will only seek out those with weak minds. Like you."

Speaking with clear, eerie calm, Libby said, "You're going to die."

"How quaint — you only get brave when it does you no good."

Ms. Sinauer turned back to the circle and knelt at the edge. "Oxorot, I call upon you on behalf of the Brotherhood of the Rising. We brought you to this world to make a fair exchange. Ignore these plebeians, and come with those who truly understand the greatness of your power." She reached forward and swept aside the salt.

"Don't do that," Irene said but did not move. She wanted to. Max could see the urge crawling across her gritting teeth. But she would not strike out. Not when Max and Libby were being held against their will. Not when Sandra continued her spell. Irene could be tough, but she wasn't an idiot. She had a duty to fulfill — watch over Sandra while she was in a meditative state. Nothing would stop Irene from seeing that done.

Max caught her eye and nodded. He wanted her to know that he understood.

When Ms. Sinauer stepped back, the purple ball stretched into the shape of a man — a faceless, purple man. It walked out of the circle, its feet several inches above the ground, and it offered its hand toward Ms. Sinauer.

Max's arm shook violently, but he didn't know if that was fear or the pain of Punk Girl's grasp. Probably both.

Ms. Sinauer dropped to her knees and bowed her head. "Please, great Oxorot, listen to our request and know that we will provide a vessel for you to walk in our world free."

Oxorot let his head drop to look down upon Ms. Sinauer. "Already have a vessel."

Max's stomach lurched. He knew what was coming. Ms.

Sinauer had to know, too. How could she not?

Drawing his mouth into a tight line, Max watched as Oxorot sauntered over to him. An odd buzz came off of its skin like failing neon tubes, and Max smelled burning in the air.

Oxorot stared at him — well, watched Max with a blank purple blob of a face. Max assumed the thing *stared.*

In its gritty voice, Oxorot said, "My vessel."

"Never."

"We'll see."

Max tried to get off a final word, but Oxorot plunged forward. Straight into Max. Again.

Chapter 33

THE SKY DARKENED as if the night had reversed course, and though Max did not move from the parking lot, everyone else had disappeared. Even the early-morning traffic and those walking to work had vanished. Only Max remained. Max and an empty city. Then he heard it —

Chop. Chop. Chop.

But the chill that sound had produced before, now filled him with fire. No matter how time stretched and twisted, no matter if this experience only lasted seconds in the real world, seconds were all they had left. He had no time for these mind games.

Chop. Chop. Chop.

"Fine," Max said as he stormed off toward the sound.

Not surprisingly, it came from the back of the parking lot — where Sandra had been casting her spell. Max edged around the front end of the old Volvo to find his father holding a now-familiar bloody ax over his head and slamming it down into Max's wife.

Seeing Sandra stopped Max from tossing a snarky comment. Not because of the gruesome horror but because of a single question — how did Oxorot get into him this time? He had been in the same space as Sandra. Whenever they were together, they shielded each other from the spirit.

Max's father wiped the sweat from his brow, leaving behind a bloodied trail. "Your faith failed you."

"Reading my mind? Aren't we beyond parlor tricks?"

"You can't deny that we're here. I guess you don't love Sandra as much as you thought. Am I lying?"

"Everything out of your mouth is a lie."

With a disappointed sigh, his father said, "Everything I have said has been true and you know it. Just because the myths and legends have built up that making a deal with a spirit is a deal with evil does not make it so. Those are just stories. I am here, humbly before you, asking to borrow your body for a short time, so that I may enjoy the bounty of this planet that you waste every day. That's all. And you? I can give you anything you want in return. But I know that your desires go far beyond what you have. You don't love your wife. Your family? They're not really anything at all. Just the convenient placeholders for the real dream wife, the real dream family you never had." He tossed the ax to Max. "There's the real answer. Cut it all down and start anew."

Max did not recall making any effort to catch the ax, but there it was in his hand. "I reject you," he said. But nothing changed.

How could nothing change? The whole idea that this spirit kept targeting him was absurd. Max unconditionally loved Sandra. They had been together since college, and his heart never stopped growing for her. They had been through wealthy times and near-homeless poverty. They had been on the verge of death and full of life. More than any couple he had ever encountered, their wedding vows had proven to be reality and not simply romantic words.

Yet something in him spoke to this spirit — made it think it could change his feelings. What could that be? What kernel of truth laid dormant, buried deep within him?

PB and J — he had great feelings for them. Though the boys were not his blood, that didn't matter. Though he and Sandra had never planned to have children, that didn't matter. He loved them. Plain and simple.

His mother, too. Sure, she annoyed the hell out of them, but that didn't stop his unconditional love for her.

So why would Oxorot keep coming at him? As Max thought each question, he swung the ax against the air. All of Oxorot's actions frustrated Max, made him feel sullied by the mere suggestion that he could be disloyal to his family. That he could dispose of them without a second glance.

"You overthink things," his father said. "Always have. It's really quite simple. It's easy to destroy the thing that causes you trouble. Much better than trying to patch it over and over in a blind faith idea that you might someday fix it. You won't. Destruction clears the way out for new things to grow. Nature understands this, why can't you?"

The heft of the ax pulled on Max's arm. He could do it. With a looping motion, he swung the ax overhead. Oxorot was right. Max walked up to the corpse of Sandra. He nodded, and out of the corner of his eye, his father flashed hungry teeth. This would work.

"That's right. That's good," his father said. "Chop with the ax and put an end to your failed life. Choose a new future. A real dream come true. Anything you want, you tell me."

"I want ..."

"Yes?"

"I want ..."

"Tell me."

"I want you out of my life." Max brought the ax down and at an angle like a reaper with a scythe. He buried the ax head into his father's gut. As his father screamed, the sound mutated into a gritty shriek — one that echoed as if they stood in a deep cave. His father's skin bubbled. It changed shade to a deep burgundy. Another cry and the shade shifted to purple.

Max blinked, and the sky lightened to its predawn colors. Sandra sat in her casting circle while Irene stood nearby. Libby and the Brotherhood remained in their positions as if nothing but a few seconds had transpired. Punk Girl still stood behind Max, but she no longer cinched his arm against his back.

They all stared at him.

Oxorot stumbled out of Max. Ms. Sinauer and the Brotherhood gasped while Sandra's lips curled upward.

With a swish of air, Oxorot folded back into its sphere form. Something about the way its surface rippled, the way it vibrated with barely contained motion — it was angry. Livid. Worse than that — it was coming for Max.

He set his feet at a firm distance, bracing for the terrible pain of those claws. If he had to take this thing on himself, then so be it. He knew who he loved. He knew what dreams mattered. And he would fight for them.

As Max rolled his fingers into tight fists, he heard a single voice cut through. A wonderful voice.

"Need a hand?" Drummond said.

Chapter 34

LIKE A PALE BLUE MISSILE, Drummond sailed forward and smashed into the purple ball. Oxorot took on a human form, shook off the attack, and lifted its arms like a pugilist from the 1920s.

"You took me by surprise before," Drummond said as he squared off. "Don't think that'll happen again. Not only am I ready for you, but I'm stronger now."

"Liar," Oxorot said. "I've drained all you have."

"I got my people here, and this time, that bond is stronger than ever."

Drummond launched ahead. Oxorot shot forward. They clashed like mountain goats and locked arms. Ghost and spirit grappled right through a van. Drummond spun Oxorot into the air, cycloning leaves around them, and soared up after it. Everyone gawked like spectators at an air show.

"You," Ms. Sinauer said to Max. "You screwed this up."

"I'm pretty good at that. Can't say I'm sorry, though. Didn't like the idea of getting possessed by that thing."

"You can be as flippant as you want, it won't change anything. Oxorot will take control of you."

"From my angle here, it looks like Drummond's kicking your little spirit boy's butt."

Right on time, Drummond hurled Oxorot into the pavement.

Ms. Sinauer approached Max. She smelled of late-night coffee, and Max stepped to the side — partly to escape her bad breath, mostly to get away from Punk Girl.

"You've named your ghost?" Ms. Sinauer said. "Is he your little pet?"

Drummond's head poked through the pavement. As his fists pummeled downward, he said, "Lady, I ain't anybody's pet."

Losing focus for a moment cost him. Four purple arms thrust upward and entangled the ghost. Max wanted to lunge forward, to help in some manner, but Ms. Sinauer barred his way.

"Are you so stupid that you don't understand what's going on here? Don't you see why we're here? Why we allowed this to go on?"

Max paused and he saw the answer snap into place. "Mr. Carroll. He ruined everything for you. He took that totem and you lost control. When we showed up at the warehouse, you weren't simply casting a spell to call up Oxorot again. You were desperate. Blood magic isn't easy and you'd already screwed it up the first time."

"I did not fail the first time. Mr. Carroll is to blame for that."

"If believing that lets you sleep better at night, then sure, we'll go with that."

"It's the truth."

Drummond burst into the air with Oxorot close behind. Max glanced up at his partner. Drummond grinned as he cocked back a fist and clocked the spirit before it could land a blow.

"The truth is that you couldn't manage to call the spirit back, but you found an alternative in us. All you had to do was sit back and wait. Either we succeeded in calling the spirit or we failed and I got possessed. You were happy regardless."

"And now we have a chance for both outcomes." With a hunger in her eyes, she said, "We won't leave here until either she —" She opened a hand toward Libby. "— or you is taken as Oxorot's vessel. It doesn't matter that your wife's spell called the spirit. We brought it into this world, so the deal to be made belongs to us. You can't steal it from the Brotherhood."

Oxorot whipped Drummond through a brick wall. As it followed up to punch, Drummond roared back, splitting the spirit in two. Even as it reformed, Drummond spun back with two more punches. Max thought Drummond had the upper-hand, but he couldn't be sure.

The candle flames brightened once more. As the flames lifted, so did the cars. All of them. The Volvo, the Ford Focus with the dented front, the freshly detailed Prius, the two vans — every vehicle in the lot rose into the air.

"W-What's going on?" Goatee said.

Max said, "You really thought we called Oxorot here to cut a deal?"

Ms. Sinauer's cocky demeanor faltered. "You can't possibly think you'll control the spirit."

"Not at all. We don't care about having its power. We're sending it back, and if it won't go," Max said, narrowing his focus entirely onto her, "then we'll destroy it."

Her face flooded red. He figured she would be angry, but the fierce rage that exploded from her shocked him. She clenched her fists and bent forward as if she could spew fire like a dragon. She howled.

Carl stormed forward — not at Max but heading toward Sandra. Max jumped in front of the man and whipped out his handgun. That stopped everybody. Even Ms. Sinauer.

Though the rattle of Drummond and Oxorot throwing each other through the floating cars capered around them, nobody on the ground moved or spoke. They stared at Max, each trying to gauge how far he would be willing to go.

"Libby, get over here," Max said. She shrugged out of Goatee's grip and hastened to Irene's side. Gesturing with the gun, Max herded the Brotherhood together. "Nobody touches my wife or our friends. Got it?"

Ms. Sinauer shrugged. "Have it your way. We'll leave. If you manage to send Oxorot back, we'll just summon him again."

"I doubt it. I've seen how difficult it is to pull this off. You barely managed the first time and you failed the second. Plus, you need the blood. How many murders do you think you can actually get away with?"

The windows on the Ford blew outward, and pebbles of safety glass rained onto the pavement. Drummond squared off once more. To Sandra, he said, "Doll, anything you can do to weaken this thing would be appreciated."

Max tried to keep his mind on holding the Brotherhood in check. Sandra knew what to do. Drummond knew what to do. They didn't need him for anything more. But Max loathed the idea that he stood in front of a crazed cult with nothing but an empty handgun — especially as a parking lot full of cars floated around him.

They made strange sounds as the shock absorbers shifted around. The metal on the beaten cars whined like animals in pain. Waves of chilled air followed by blasts of heat rolled down from above. Max even caught electricity arcing between a few cars — not much, not yet. If this spell went on too long, though, he suspected they would all risk electrocution on top of possession and plain old death.

From behind, Sandra called out, and Max's stomach flipped at what he heard. She yelled as if caught in a torrential downpour. Her voice sounded strained, tearful — walking the edge between great suffering and great success.

"Irene!" she said. "I need you!"

Irene moved out of Max's sight, presumably to help Sandra. He heard them talk to each other but could not make out the words. He heard Drummond grunt as the ghost took a punch or maybe threw one, Max couldn't take his eyes off the Brotherhood to check.

Ms. Sinauer's gloating smile sickened him. "Hurts, doesn't it? They're all doing the important things, and you're stuck babysitting. It's like they don't even need you. I mean, even Libby could hold a gun on us. You really are superfluous."

"Shut up," Max said. "I've heard enough of that crap from Oxorot, and it didn't provoke me to make a deal with him. You've got nothing to offer over that thing, so save your breath."

"I'm not trying to deal, and I'm not trying to convince you of anything. I'm merely pointing out how you've failed as much as I have. More, even. At least, my team still supports me. They still need me. You — you're not much of a leader, are you?"

Max rolled his head to ease the muscles in his neck. He knew it was all lies. He knew his value to the team. There were plenty of cases in which he found himself at the center of it all. But this time, Sandra and Drummond had it well in hand. He only needed to support them, and that was fine.

So why did Ms. Sinauer think she could provoke him with these taunts?

A short yelp came from behind — Max thought Irene had made the sound — and the electrical arcs between the floating vehicles increased. A mass of pale blue and purple tumbled across Max's view. He flexed his fingers around the handgun as he fought the urge to watch Drummond's fight. No matter what, he had to stop the Brotherhood.

But then a dark hole formed in the air behind Ms. Sinauer's people. An Audi shifted out of the way, scratching up against the Prius. All in the Brotherhood spun around and arched back to watch this sudden change.

The quiet surrounding the hole punctured through all the noise and shut it down. Every last sound. From Sandra's mumbled spellcasting to Drummond and Oxorot tossing each other through cars and walls, from the growing number of footsteps, phone conversations, and passing cars to Max's own heartbeat pounding in his ears. For five solid seconds — an eternity — not a single sound escaped this hole as if somebody had turned the volume down on existence.

With Sandra's voice and the firm conviction behind it, the audio of the world returned. She said, "Drummond, throw Oxorot in there. Send that bastard home."

Ms. Sinauer whirled back. "No," she whispered, though the hatred in her tone reached Max with no problem. Her left cheek twitched as her entire body tensed. With a full-throated screech, she bellowed words Max did not want to hear. "Stop them. Now!"

Ignoring the possibility of getting shot, all three of Ms. Sinauer's accomplices launched forward. Max pointed his handgun from Goatee to Punk Girl to Carl, but none of them reacted. They did not care. Or they accepted the risks. Or — it didn't matter. Max held an empty weapon. Whether they knew it or not, the Brotherhood had called his bluff.

Well, he had his fists, his feet, and his training. That was no bluff.

Twisting from the waist and lashing out with as much speed as he could generate, Max kicked to the side and caught Carl in the hip. That knocked the big man down — mostly due to the surprise of being hit, but Max would take any win. Without waiting for a reaction, he spun on Goatee, throwing a wild punch that should have missed but raked across Goatee's chest. Punk Girl pulled back a step. She raised her fists with competence.

Max had been lucky with the first two men, and that luck made him look like a badass. It gave Punk Girl pause. He hoped he could use that to his advantage. Especially because he felt her strength earlier when she had locked his arm. If she got the better of him now, she might send him to the hospital.

Uttering an attempt at a warrior cry, Irene barreled into Punk Girl. She never stopped moving. Though small, she packed a whollop. Punk Girl had been so focused on Max, so taken by surprise at this older woman, that she reacted too slowly. When she hit the ground, her head bumped the pavement hard enough to daze her.

Irene did not wait for results. After mowing down her adversary, she pivoted and charged Goatee. Max knew that left Carl — the big, muscular Carl.

Taking a page from Irene, Max rushed Carl, jumped into the air and stuck out his foot. Not a perfect flying side kick, but it did well enough. He smashed in Carl's body and they both fell to the ground. From there, a wrestling match ensued.

Carl had strength, but Max had speed. Whenever the big man reached for Max's legs or arms, Max managed to evade the grapple. But while Max could twist and spin, he failed to accomplish anything more. And he knew nobody could escape every attack forever. Eventually, Carl would get hold and pin Max down. Then the punches would follow.

As Max tried to find a clear path forward, he heard Ms.

Sinauer's disgusting laugh. "Thank you," she said, dropping to her knees and gazing up at Oxorot. "All your fighting has created the energy the spirit needs. And now that the sun has risen, you have lost."

Her words pierced the brawling. Max and Carl both stopped to listen and then lifted their eyes skyward. The red and orange of dawn already faded to the brighter day. Oxorot displayed a deeper, richer purple, and it moved faster than before.

And Drummond — Oxorot held Drummond against the hood of the Volvo with one hand while four more claws took jabs at his ghost flesh.

Ms. Sinauer stood and approached the casting circle. Irene spat from the ground — Goatee had his knee on her back and kept her from moving. Ms. Sinauer strolled ahead, overflowing with arrogance. Max wanted to tackle her, keep her away from Sandra, but Carl's meaty hand clamped around Max's wrist.

Ms. Sinauer kicked a wider gap in the salt and stepped forward. "You can stop wasting your energy on this spell. It's over."

Little bits of light flashed around the edges of the hole gaping in the air. Sandra's face tightened as she forced herself to concentrate. The lights disappeared.

"There's no point, witch. Oxorot will take its vessel, and we will see that you all pay for the trouble you have caused."

Sandra opened her eyes and glared up while keeping her head low. "You keep your hands off my family."

Without moving a muscle, Sandra's body lifted off the ground. Like the cars, she floated several feet high. She snarled, and Ms. Sinauer stepped back.

"Now, Libby!" Sandra said.

From behind them all, Libby burst forth carrying a length of metal pipe. She swung hard at the backs of Ms. Sinauer's knees. A pain-drenched cry and Ms. Sinauer fell to the pavement. But Libby did not stop there. With wild eyes and an animalistic call, she whirled around, hammering the pipe against the woman's arm. Ms. Sinauer bent over, holding her wound as Libby lifted the pipe overhead like an ax.

"Stop!" Max said.

Libby froze.

"Don't do this. If you kill her, Oxorot wins. You'll give the spirit the strength and the opening — it'll possess you."

Breathing heavy, Libby held the pipe and glowered at Ms. Sinauer. "She killed Angie and Gene."

"I know. And she'll pay for her crimes."

Ms. Sinauer laughed. "I won't. They'll never convict me. The Brotherhood will see that I remain free."

"Don't listen," Max said.

"You can't stop me. I'll find some other naïve idiots and use their blood like I did to your friends." Ms. Sinauer closed her eyes.

"She's goading you. Don't listen. She wants you to strike her."

"Go on, Libby. I've killed people. I tried to kill you. I ordered my followers to do the same. I'll do it again. You're the only one with a weapon. You're the only one who can stop me."

"Be quiet," Max snapped. "Dying won't get you anywhere."

Ms. Sinauer said, "It'll be the ultimate burst of negative energy. It'll free Oxorot completely."

"Shut up!" Libby backed off, pacing like a trapped tiger, tears streaming into her nose and mouth.

Max wanted to lunge forward and snatch that pipe away. If Libby hurt Ms. Sinauer, if she killed the woman, then it would be the same as if he had taken the ax to his wife. It would open Libby up to Oxorot's possession.

Banging the pipe against the van and leaving a dent, Libby spun back at Max. "She's a murderer."

"I know."

"They're all murderers."

"Don't let them turn you into one, too."

All grew still as the world pinpointed right on Libby. Even Drummond and Oxorot held quiet long enough to see the outcome.

Libby raised the pipe once more and swung it down. Hard.

Chapter 35

MS. SINAUER COULD NOT HELP HERSELF. Human instincts took over. She cringed and cried out, "No! Don't kill me!"

The pipe clanged on the pavement next to Ms. Sinauer. Railing in frustration, Libby shook her fists in the air and yelled until her voice cracked and her body slumped over. Max watched Ms. Sinauer closely, but her sense of self-preservation kept her mouth shut. In fact, Max noticed that everybody watched her. For a long moment, nobody struggled against another. Nobody threw a punch or screamed out in pain. Only Libby's sobbing filled the air.

Goatee pushed off Irene and then helped her stand. His eyes never left Ms. Sinauer. Punk Girl stayed on her hands and knees, too absorbed in her aching head to notice much else. Carl looked as if his idol had turned out to be a bastard that hated her fans.

"You lied to us," Carl said.

Ms. Sinauer shook her head as tears formed. "No. Never."

"You said if any of us could sacrifice to the spirit, we would be rewarded. You said it was a great honor that the Brotherhood would never forget."

"Yes, yes. That's all true."

"Then why did you beg her to stop?"

She had no answer.

Max's chest lifted. Nobody fought. Nobody yelled at another or sought the destruction of another. All the attacks, all the crazed back and forth, all of it had ceased. Max did not feel tension between any of them. During this pause, all the negative energy had gone. Only for this moment, but in this singular space, it had collectively vanished.

Before he could voice the idea, Drummond caught his eye and gave Max a knowing wink. He wrapped an arm around Oxorot's purple neck and pounded on its head. The spirit tried to wrest free, but it only had the sunlight to give it energy. After all they had gone through that night, sunlight would never come close to matching the sheer force of Drummond and Sandra. Never.

Punk Girl wobbled to her feet but would be no problem to handle. Carl might as well have been a six-year-old the way he stared at Ms. Sinauer with disbelief. He had built a worldview that crumbled before him. Max only worried about Goatee. But Irene glared up at the man, and he simply shook his head. They were all done.

Uttering a loud groan, Drummond pushed Oxorot toward the hole in the air. With a kick in the backside, he sent the spirit through. The hole snapped shut.

All the cars dropped to the ground. Windows cracked as shock absorbers failed to take on the brutal fall. Two horns sounded and one tire burst.

Sandra dropped, too.

Max rushed to her side. Cradling her, he kissed her sweat-soaked forehead. "You did good. No, you did great."

In the exhausted silence, Libby walked over to Ms. Sinauer. She bent down and picked up the pipe, dragging it into her hand to create a long, ear-grating noise. Ms. Sinauer covered her face as she cried. Libby watched and shook her head.

"I can't believe I almost committed murder over you." She set her foot on Ms. Sinauer's shoulder and thrust outward. Ms. Sinauer fell over, offering no resistance.

The steady plinks of a cane arrived from the corner of the lot. Max did not bother to look. He already knew that sound too well.

Mr. Carroll walked up the middle of the lot. Across the street, a man and a woman observed from the shadows. Max presumed they were the ones who had busted Mr. Carroll free from Irene's guard.

As Mr. Carroll swaggered in, he nodded at Punk Girl,

inclined his head toward Irene, and halted behind Ms. Sinauer. Max traded glares with the man leaning on his cane, and though he knew Mr. Carroll could not see Drummond, Max liked the fact that Drummond descended next to Sandra with his hat pulled low and his fists at the ready.

"It certainly seems that all y'all have had quite an impressive evening." Mr. Carroll made sure to lock eyes with each member of the Brotherhood. "Unfortunately, you failed. You let this ridiculous hodge-podge of a team defeat you. What a shame."

Goatee said, "We were following her orders."

"And that did not fare well, did it? I came to y'all on numerous occasions to offer my help and expertise, yet I was rejected each and every time. Even after I showed that I could take control of the spirit — something Ms. Sinauer never properly did — yet she still saw fit to exclude me. Now, now, don't worry, Mr. Blake, I don't blame you."

Goatee looked relieved. "Thank you."

Max felt less relieved. He did not like anything Mr. Carroll said, and he liked even less having to rewire his naming. Not Goatee but Mr. Blake.

"First things first, however," Mr. Carroll said as he approached Ms. Sinauer. "You have attempted to lead this historic and worthy organization, and your leadership has been found wanting. I'm afraid your time with the Brotherhood of the Rising has come to an end."

Covering her face, Ms. Sinauer shuddered. Before Max could do more than open his mouth, Mr. Carroll pulled out a small revolver and fired it into Ms. Sinauer's head. Irene and Libby both let out short, shocked utterances but neither dared to move. Max, however, eased Sandra to the ground and got his feet under, ready to pounce forward.

Drummond said, "Don't play the hero. Not now."

Max risked glancing at Drummond. He raised a questioning eyebrow.

"You're watching a regime change. I've seen it many times over the last century. It's never pretty. But I can tell you this — right now, those Brotherhood members are adrift. They don't know what to do, so they're not doing anything. If you go running at Mr. Carroll, throwing fists and screaming bloody murder, it'll galvanize them. After all that's happened tonight, I suspect they'll take out every last frustration upon you, Sandra, and the two fine ladies. None of you will survive."

Max bowed his head.

"Cheer up, partner. Just because Mr. Carroll got what he wanted and is now leader of the Brotherhood doesn't mean he succeeded or that we failed. We know who our enemy is now. That's something he would prefer to have kept hidden."

With a curt motion of his hands, Mr. Carroll ordered Carl and Punk Girl to clean up the mess. Carl lifted Ms. Sinauer's lifeless body and set it aside while Punk Girl gathered any evidence from the ground. Goatee hustled to the sidewalk, fishing out his keys as he headed off. Max knew that soon enough, they would back a car into the parking lot, dump everything they could into the trunk — including the body — and that would be the end of it.

Libby could try going to the police, but what could she say? Yes, she had witnessed a murder; however, all traces of Angie and Gene as well as any indication of the warehouse being used for a spell would be long gone. The police would only find a dusty, empty building.

They really can get away with murder.

As dark as that thought was, another thought — one far worse in Max's opinion — struck him. "This was all planned," he blurted out.

"Heavens, no," Mr. Carroll said. "I'm flattered you think so highly of my abilities, but I assure you, I could never have come up with such complicated machinations. Frankly, nobody is that intelligent. Far too many variables. But I do know how to make the most of an opportunity."

"And we're that opportunity?"

"Most certainly. I had hoped for the spirit to possess one of you — likely would have killed the rest — and I would have used that victory to gain membership to the Brotherhood. But here you are, fighting back in such unexpected ways. All along you undermined Ms. Sinauer so brilliantly, well that I hardly had to work. What I had planned would've taken a few years, but you did most of it for me in one night. Thank you."

Max put on his most threatening glare. "I know you won't listen to me, but trust me on this — you do not want to get involved with magic in this city. It won't end well for you."

"Why? Because of the Hulls? Because of you and your wife? That's all over. The witches are in disarray, the Hulls are a pale imitation of their former power, and you — well, you're just a gnat to these groups. In fact, the more I look at it, and I have looked at it quite extensively, I can guarantee that this is the perfect time for the Brotherhood to make itself known." Goatee — apparently, Mr. Blake — pulled up in a dark van. Tapping his cane on the ground, Mr. Carroll went on, "I suggest you rouse your wife, gather your friends, and leave. We'll clean up this mess. Consider it our professional courtesy. And let's hope we never cross paths again. You won't receive such gentle hands the next time."

"Best to get moving," Drummond said. "We stopped the spirit. Let this guy have his moment. We'll get him eventually."

Though it burned in his gut, Max agreed. He helped Sandra to her feet. She needed some assistance walking but every passing minute brought her a little closer to full consciousness. As they reached the sidewalk, Drummond scouted ahead, making sure they did not bump into any law enforcement or other parties that might take notice. Irene and Libby followed behind. Max looked, but the man and the woman in the shadows were gone.

Seconds later, they walked among the morning bustle, and nobody paid them any attention. Nobody cared. They were nothing more than a group of people moving too slow for those who had to get to work.

Chapter 36

WHEN THEY REACHED THE PARKING GARAGE, Irene put her hand out to stop everyone. "I think we should part ways here. I'll call a rideshare to get my car, and Libby, if you want to join me, I'll get you on your way."

"My way?" Libby's voice cracked.

"Yes, dear. That is, well, I assumed you still desired to leave this city. And the state, for that matter. Don't you have a boyfriend and a job and a whole life to get back to?"

Though Libby nodded, Max could see the truth in her eyes — those normal things felt so far removed from her, they might as well have been on Mars. Irene put a motherly arm around Libby. They leaned into each other.

"Okay," Libby said, but Max wondered if she even knew what she had agreed to do. Still, he trusted that Irene wouldn't simply dump Libby. She would make sure the young lady had a place to go and somebody to pick her up when she arrived. Libby had many years of therapy ahead of her. But despite her lost expression at the moment, Max had seen this woman's strength, confidence, and businesslike organization to her life. He suspected that in a few days, she would start putting things back together. She would be haunted by the murders she had witnessed, but in the end, she would survive and possibly do far better. Not the outcome he wanted for any of them, but better than dying back at that parking lot.

As Irene ushered Libby up the street, Sandra tugged on Max's sleeve. "Let's go get the boys."

"No, hon. You're going to bed. I'll get the boys."

"But I —"

"You can barely stand."

"I need to see them."

"You will. When you wake up in a few hours. But you were the hero today, and the hero gets to rest when the bad guys are defeated."

"Mr. Carroll wasn't defeated."

"Oxorot was. Now, shush. We're going to the car, I'm taking you home, and you go to sleep."

He could see the desire to argue pushing against the lovely idea of sleep. Sleep won out.

As Max drove away, he made sure to go around the block so he could see the office. The street had been cordoned off, but the answer was clear enough — the days of their office on Trade Street were over. Considering their financial situation, he did not see them having any office space in the near-future — they had barely managed this one.

"Sad to see that place go," Drummond said, floating in the backseat.

"Yeah. I really wish we had some insurance."

"I wish I had a bookshelf to call home. Think I'll go hang my hat in the Other for a bit. There are a few nice gals that have always offered a soft place to lay my head. After fighting that spirit, I feel a strong need to rest."

Rest sounded great. Max's muscles ached — all of them. Bruises along his spine throbbed with every motion, and his head threatened a migraine if he didn't get some sleep soon.

He checked the rearview mirror. "You going to be okay?"

"Oh, sure. It'll take a lot more than that to stop me."

"I'm glad to hear it."

Max headed along the busy streets, watched the people hustling through their lives, and knew that few of them ever understood what was important. But he had nearly lost everything this past night. He knew.

He cleared his throat. "Listen, I got something to say."

"No need." Drummond made sure to be looking out the side window.

"It's important that —"

With a frustrated sigh, the ghost said, "There's a lot I can say about progress in the world, a lot of good, but emotionally, I prefer the way things were back in my day. You didn't need to express everything with words and sappy talk. You knew how people felt by the things they did — and the occasional embarrassing outburst."

"Okay, then," Max said. "I won't say anything."

"I appreciate it."

"When you come back from your vacation in the Other, we'll have a bookcase built-in to our living room. It's all yours."

Drummond lowered his hat but he could not hide. "That's more like it."

An hour later, Max had deposited Sandra in their bed and watched Drummond vanish for the Other. He sacrificed five minutes to microwave the dregs of coffee from the day before and give himself a final caffeine boost. Then back in the car, he headed to his mother's apartment to pick up the boys.

On the radio, the morning news told him everything he needed to hear. The office fire had been pegged to old wiring. Thankfully, since the building only supported businesses, nobody was inside so late at night. Not a single injury. A few blocks away, vandals ruined an entire parking lot full of cars. And on the same street there were odd reports of electrical disturbances, people seeing floating cars, and even one person claiming she witnessed a cult ceremony. Other than the vandalism, police found no evidence of anything out of the ordinary. City departments were deployed to check into a possible gas leak that might have caused hallucinations.

Max chuckled. "Every time."

When he arrived at the apartment, he bounded up to the door like a kid excited to be home from an excruciating day at school. He rang the doorbell and knocked on the door. When his mother opened, he walked right in and grabbed the nearest boy — J — into a hug.

PB entered from the kitchen, drinking soda from the can. "What's with you?"

"Nothing," Max said. "Get over here."

"No thanks. I'm not in need of a hug."

"Quit being a teen and get over here."

PB reluctantly entered into the group hug. When Max finally let them loose, he inhaled their scent and let a long sense of relief wash over.

"What happened to you?" Mrs. Porter said. "Are you okay?"

Max patted the boys on the shoulders. "Go get your stuff together. I need to talk with your grandmother."

PB shrugged but J held Max's gaze a little longer. Not for the first time, Max thought that boy really did see more than he let on.

Once the Sandwich Boys had vacated the room, Mrs. Porter sat on the edge of her old sofa. "You're worrying me. What's going on?"

Max knelt before his mother and kissed her cheek. "I'm glad you're concerned."

"Of course I'm concerned. You're my son."

"I know. But things have been rather cold between us for a while."

"You want to talk about this now?"

Pushing aside a copy of *Southern Living,* Max sat on the corner of the coffee table. "We had a very hard night, and it got me thinking about you."

"Difficult things make you think of me? Wonderful."

"Not like that. Look, I know we have issues to work out, and we will. That's what I want to say. I love you. You're my family, and I want to be at ease with you. I'm reaching out to you right now, right here. Please. Reach back."

Tears welled in her eyes. "You are such a silly boy. I've been sitting here waiting for you to get your head out of the ground. Reach back? I've never stopped reaching out to you."

The old instinct to argue her version of reality rushed up Max's throat, but he swallowed it down. "I'm taking the boys home, and then I need to sleep. But I'd like to come back tonight."

"That'd be lovely. I'll make some dinner for us."

"Fine. But you'll want a bottle of wine with whatever you make."

"Oh?"

"I want to have the best version of a family I can have. In order to do that, I need to make peace with you."

She frowned. "Isn't that what we're doing?"

"Yes, but there's more. It's time for me to put to rest the things that have troubled me from growing up. It's time for me to understand and let go of those things so I can be what the boys need." Placing his hand on top of hers, he said, "It's time we talk about my father."

Mrs. Porter let out a nervous titter. "We might need two bottles of wine for that."

Max laughed. The boys walked by with their bags and watched with quizzical looks that sent Max and his mother into hysterics. Dabbing at the tears in his eyes, Max got up and ushered the boys toward the car.

Between Sandra, the boys, his mother and Drummond, Max really had a great family. One might even say perfect.

Afterword

I suspect you folks will already know that the Reynolda House sections of this book are nearly 100% true and accurate. Back when I was working on *Southern Fury,* my mother and step-father came for a visit. Looking for something interesting to do, we decided to visit Reynolda House for a day. I had always intended to do so, and this made a great opportunity.

The instant we arrived, I knew I would eventually be using the space in a Max Porter book. I just didn't expect to dive into it so soon. But with COVID 19 locking the world down, I no longer had an easy way to drive around Winston-Salem to follow up on whatever locations I wanted to use. But I had all my notes about Reynolda House, and I still had the Reynolda House app on my phone which contained video of the family, photos of every room, and pictures of many of the objects and art to be found throughout the house. So, between those and my memory, plus a bit of artistic license when necessary, I rebuilt the estate for Max and the gang to explore. If you ever visit Winston-Salem, I highly recommend checking out this incredible place. It's amazing.

The other historical references to local murders and such ugliness are all true — especially when I'm directly quoting from newspaper articles. Most everything else in the book is fiction. However, as a side note, the office building across from the YMCA has always been a parking lot. From the very first book, Drummond's original office was something I created. I always planned for it to revert back to reality, and so I'm happy to finally get around to making that happen. Possibly the only time in my life I'll be excited about writing a parking lot.

Acknowledgements

Like most authors, I often begin this section by noting that no book is written in a vacuum, and while that's certainly still true, this book came as close as possible thanks to COVID 19 scouring the Earth. Being in lockdown meant that I had far less contact with my fellow writers and others who often have no idea that they are helping contribute to the completion of a novel. In fact, more than ever before, it was you fans who kept me going on this one. As you devoured the older books in the series, you gave me that extra push to find the next page and the next and the next. Special thanks must go to my mother and step-father, of course. If you read the Afterword, you know that their last visit led to the impetus for this tale. And I always have room to thank my wife and son. Y'all have no clue how many errors, typos, continuity mistakes, etc, they've fixed before these books ever reach your hands.

About the Author

Stuart Jaffe is the madman behind *The Max Porter Paranormal Mysteries,* the *Nathan K* thrillers, *The Parallel Society* series, *The Malja Chronicles, The Bluesman, Founders, Real Magic,* and so much more. His unique brand of old pulp adventure mixed with a contemporary sensibility brings out the best in a variety of SF/F sub-genres. He trained in martial arts for over a decade until a knee injury ended that practice. Now, he plays lead guitar in a local blues band, *The Bootleggers,* and enjoys life on a small farm in rural North Carolina. For those who continue to keep count, the animal list is as follows: one dog, two cats, two aquatic turtles, and fifteen chickens. The horse is now at a new pasture. She's having a wonderful time hanging with a herd of thirty other horses. Much better for her. As best as he's been able to manage, Stuart has made sure that the chickens do not live in the house.

www.ingramcontent.com/pod-product-compliance
Lightning Source LLC
Chambersburg PA
CBHW030520310726
48979CB00010B/1739/J

9781963517064